THE CHINESE BOX

Dimitri Johnston, half Russian and half English, has spent most of his life in Hong Kong, where he is now a university lecturer, and it is in Hong Kong that he feels most at home. But his English wife, Helen, is growing more and more estranged from Dimitri and from a place and people she neither likes nor understands. Then Dimitri meets Mila, a Chinese dancer who is in Hong Kong hoping to get a visa to allow her to join a ballet group in London. As their relationship deepens, Dimitri and Mila find themselves entangled in the troubled political affairs of Britain's last great colony, when it shudders under the waves of the Cultural Revolution spreading out from China. In the outcome, Dimitri has to accept that life is indeed a Chinese box: complex, puzzling and often empty in the end.

Books by Christopher New

Goodbye Chairman Mao

The China Coast Trilogy
Shanghai
The Chinese Box
A Change of Flag

Philosophy of Literature: An Introduction

THE CHINESE BOX

Christopher New

An Orchid Pavilion Book
Asia 2000 Limited
Hong Kong

© 2001 Christopher New
All Rights Reserved

ISBN: 962–8783–06–8

An Orchid Pavilion Book
Published by Asia 2000 Ltd
Fifth Floor, 31A Wyndham Street
Central Hong Kong

http://www.asia2000.com.hk

Typeset in Adobe Garamond by Asia 2000 Ltd
Printed in Hong Kong by Editions Quaille

First Printing 2001

Printing History

W.H Allen edition, 1975

Hong Kong
The Year of the Ram

The man got out of the bed first. He was fair-skinned, with thick, dark hair curling over his chest and belly. Drops of sweat glistened on his skin and trickled down between the hairs.

He walked to the grimy little window and pushed it open, leaning forward to look out. The harsh glare of the afternoon sunlight dazzled the eyes of the Chinese girl watching him from the bed. She sat up, frowning. Her long black hair hung down to her shoulder blades. She was slim, with the small-breasted suppleness of Cantonese women. There were bruises from the man's teeth on her shoulders and arms. She looked down at them, stroking them delicately with her finger-tips. Her nails were long and varnished.

'You should be more gentle.' She spoke in Cantonese, thoughtfully rather than complainingly.

'Yes, I know.' He spoke in Cantonese too, almost faultlessly.

The room was at the top of the building. By leaning out and looking right, the man could see the airport, with its runway stretching out into the harbour, and the hills of Hong Kong Island beyond. He was watching a plane drifting down to land, skimming now over the junks and ferries which plied across the harbour. A spurt of smoke flew up as the wheels touched the runway.

The deep-throated growl of the four jet engines sounded loudly over the din of traffic in the streets below.

The girl got out of the bed too and stood looking down at the sheet, still fingering her bruises. The bed was made of bare wooden boards, with a hard kapok mattress laid on top. The sheet was stained and rumpled. She looked at it consideringly for some time, then sighed and pulled it off.

She walked across to the man, tossing her hair back over her shoulders, and leant against him. There were long thin red scratches from her nails down his back. She smiled, rubbing her check against them.

'Better not turn your back on your wife tonight.'

'*You* should be more gentle then, Julie.' He pulled her round in front of him, so that she too could look out of the window. His hand slid up her belly to cover her breast.

'I saw you yesterday.' She wriggled her buttocks against him temptingly. 'With your children.'

'Where?'

'At the beach. Shek O Wan.'

'Oh. Why didn't you say hallo?'

She stopped wriggling and glanced back at him over her shoulder. 'What would your wife have thought?'

'She wasn't there.'

'Or your children?'

'I would have told them you were one of my students at the university.'

'Sure,' she laughed, a low guttural chuckle. 'I look like one, don't I?' She started wriggling again. 'Men only say hallo to bar-girls at night.'

He was not responding to her wriggling. Her hand felt for him behind her buttocks. 'You tired?'

'No. Thinking.'

'Thinking what?'

He rested his chin on her head and breathed out slowly, blowing at the fine strands of her hair. 'Oh ... I don't know.' He shrugged, 'I'd better phone my wife.'

He dressed quickly and unlocked the door. At the end of the dark, smelly corridor, a middle-aged Chinese in shorts and singlet was shouting into the phone, a toothpick jammed between his teeth. Seeing the European coming, he hung up abruptly and gestured to him with an affable gold-toothed smile.

He'll take a cut of the money I give her, the man thought. He watched his fingers dialling his home number on Hong Kong Island. I suppose I ought to feel disgusted.

The ringing tone purr-purred for a long time in his ear. At last a woman's voice answered flatly in English.

'Helen, what time is the concert?' He could hear the squealing of the children playing or fighting.

'You know that. Eight o'clock.'

'Okay. I'll be back by seven.'

He heard a child screeching near the phone. The woman shouted back fiercely.

'What's going on?' he asked.

'Oh, the usual squabbling, that's all. The same as always.' Her voice was flat and heavy again. 'Can't you get back earlier?'

'I'm at a meeting, I'll try...'

'All right. Goodbye.'

When he came back, the girl was dressed in trousers and a sleeveless blouse. She was still looking out of the window. The sound of a police siren wailed up into the room, mournful and yet sinister.

'What's that for?' He spoke in Cantonese again.

She moved aside to let him see.

In the street below, a line of riot police were advancing with drawn batons on a crowd of workers. The sun shone on the glossy, black helmets of the police. The workers were chanting and shouting as they were pressed back. A group of them in white shirts waving red books tried to break out of the police cordon. The man watched the police batons rise and fall. To him, up there, they were soundless. One of the workers fell to his knees, was pulled up and dragged to a police van. He was still waving his red book. Another was led away, arms twisted behind his back. Everything seemed to happen slowly and quietly, as if the people below were only children's puppets moving on clumsily operated strings.

'Those are the strikers from the Artificial Flower Factory, aren't they?'

She nodded. 'I used to work there before I became a bar-girl. Bad pay, no good.'

'Sweat shop to the world,' the man said, in English.

'Uh?'

But he only shook his head, returning to Cantonese, 'You know what those red books are they're holding?'

'Sure. Chairman Mao.'

'Have you got one?'

'Me?' She laughed her guttural laugh again. 'I can't read. You can read Chinese better than me.'

'It's my job. Besides, I was born here, after all.'

She turned round and leant against him. 'You going now?'

'Yes.' He took a hundred-dollar bill out of his pocket and slipped it inside her blouse. 'Buy yourself something nice.'

As usual, she didn't demean herself by thanking him. 'I'll go and see the fortune-teller first.'

He took her fine-boned hand in his. 'You still believe all that, Julie?'

'Sometimes it comes true.'

He looked down at her hand. With its small palm and long, slender tapering fingers, it might have graced a princess in Europe. In the east, such delicacy was too commonplace. '*I'll* tell you your fortune.'

'Go on, then.'

He pored over the lines, lifting and turning her hand. It lay lightly, passively, in his large, pink, European grasp, almost like a child's. 'If you go on being a bar-girl for much longer, you'll end up in a brothel in the Walled City and die before you're thirty.'

She started to laugh, but he turned her to the window again. 'See? That way you can see the Walled City.'

She looked away from the police and the strikers to the little cluster of buildings, two hundred years old, which marked the entrance to the old walled city. Not even the police dared go in there, except in groups.

'A girl there costs five dollars and every one of them's a drug addict. They don't live long.'

This time she did laugh, pulled her hand away from his. 'No sweat,' she spoke in bar-girl English now, mocking him. 'Old woman no good. Better be dead. Not like flower worker, make two dollars a day.'

Down below, the sirens were still wailing and strikers were still being pulled one by one into the police vans. A ragged crowd was looking on in silence, neither hostile nor friendly, but with deep, impassive interest, as if, however fascinating the spectacle was, it did not ultimately concern them.

'Why on earth not, Helen?'

'It's too late, I don't feel like it now. It's too much trouble.'

'Of course it's not too late. I mean all you have to do is get dressed and —'

'I'm tired, I don't feel like it any more.'

' — Get dressed and get in the car. Is that too much?'

'The children aren't even in bed yet.'

'What do we have an amah for, for Christ's sake? *I'll* put them to bed if you like. You only have to get dressed and fix your hair.'

'I'm fed up, Dimitri, can't you understand? I'm just fed up! I don't want to go out! I don't want to do anything!'

'Can't you understand that's just why you ought to go to the bloody concert? Schwarzkopf comes here about once every five years and you specially asked me to get the tickets and now you want to behave like a spoilt child and mope around at home. Why?'

'Can't you understand that I'm just fed up?'

'Oh God, when were you ever anything else?'

They were late. Dimitri did not notice the stencilled slip inside the programme until they had settled into their seats.

Owing to an indisposition Miss Schwarzkopf has been compelled to cancel her visit at short notice. Miss Shirley Leung, the well-known local soprano, has kindly consented to take her place.

A long exasperated sigh from Helen told him she had read her slip at the same time. She sighed again, her lips tightening.

'Do you want to leave?' He shrugged apologetically. 'I'm sorry.'

'I don't care.' She leant back, closing her eyes and shaking her head.

He watched her covertly, the tightened lines at the corners of her lips, her pale cheeks and discontented frown, the shadowy throbbing of her pulse in her throat. Her long dark lashes that had once delighted him were quivering as though holding back tears. She's on the verge of a breakdown, he thought helplessly, and then, She always has been. He looked away at the stage, where the grand piano stood expectantly between two Chinese vases filled with lilies. The words of the last telegram of her musical career printed themselves across his mind. *Can you play Edinburgh next Friday?* They had left England a week before the cable was sent. It had reached them eight weeks later in Hong Kong crumpled and useless. How many years was that now?

Helen's eyes were still closed when the restrained ripple of applause with which Hong Kong audiences greeted anyone and everyone announced the appearance of the singer and her accompanist.

'Would you like to leave?' he asked her again at the interval.

She shook her head. 'Might as well be miserable here as anywhere else.' Her voice had resumed the tone of sullen resignation that he had heard on the phone in the afternoon.

'A breath of air, then.'

They went silently down the stairs into the noisy, restless foyer and then out on to the waterfront, both involved in their own solitary thoughts.

The May night air was hot and thick. Across the harbour, the lights of Kowloon glistened in the clammy dark. Dimitri, listening to the choppy waves slapping against the pier, began looking for the tall and shabby apartment block beyond the airport where Julie lived. Soft, loose-piled clouds drifting over the Kowloon hills glowed faintly translucent with the lights of the city.

Helen took out a cigarette. He lit it for her. She moved away and leant against the railing, smoking in quick shallow puffs, almost as though she were panting for breath. Her eyes gazed across the harbour, blank and brooding. A ragged little Chinese boy stared at them curiously for some minutes, then spat into the water and walked away.

Going back up the stairs to the hall, Dimitri heard his name called. Peter Frankam, as dapper now as when they had been undergraduates together at Cambridge.

'Not much of a substitute for Schwarzkopf, eh?' Peter looked at Helen rather than Dimitri.

She smiled brittly and looked away.

'I suppose you can't expect more in Hong Kong,' Dimitri said lamely, to cover the awkwardness.

Peter eyed them smilingly, his tongue flicking across his lips. 'How are you, Helen?' His voice was suave, almost patronising. 'Haven't seen you for years it seems ... You're looking as beautiful as ever, I must say ... More beautiful, even...'

Helen shrugged and barely smiled again. Peter's oily manners had always irritated her. She had never suspected it might be real admiration that prompted this extravagant attentiveness.

'He's still got a yen for you.' Dimitri tried to warm her with a touch of forced flippancy as they sat down again.

But she was too deep to hear or care.

After the second song, which seemed to strain the singer's voice, an attendant walked onto the stage and whispered to her. At first she seemed not to understand, but then she nodded briefly and led her accompanist off into the wings. A faint sense of unease hushed the audience, and then a man's voice sounded slowly and distinctly through the loudspeakers, first in English then in Cantonese.

'The commissioner of police announces that a curfew has been declared in certain areas of Kowloon to enable the police to deal with disturbances which are a threat to law and order. The curfew is from 11 p.m. until 4 a.m. in the following areas: Hunghom, Kowloon Tong, San Po Kong and Wong Tai Sin. If you live in these areas you are advised to return home immediately. Unless you have urgent business, you must not be on the streets in these areas between 11 p.m. tonight and 4 a.m. tomorrow.'

Helen and Dimitri sat still while all around them seats flipped back and people filed silently to the doors. At last they too stood up.

'What's that all about?' Helen was emerging from her depression. Her voice expressed some interest.

'San Po Kong is where the flower workers are striking.'

They went down towards the foyer, already nearly empty. Dimitri remembered the sunlight gleaming on the glossy black helmets of the riot police and the soundless clubbing of their batons.

'There's Elena's ballet teacher,' Helen stopped halfway down the stairs.

'Where?'

She was standing in the foyer, a tall Chinese girl in black silk trousers and a black blouse, with an orange headband round her forehead.

'She looks rather trendy.'

'I don't want to meet her.'

'We can't just walk past her.'

She had already smiled at them. Helen smiled, hesitated, then introduced Dimitri. Her name was Mila Chan. Unlike most Chinese women's, her hand was firm when he shook it, instead of lying limp and passive in his.

'I do not think we have met before?' she said.

'No.'

'Your daughter is like you.'

'Poor kid.'

She smiled. 'I did not mean that.' She spoke English without elisions or slurs, so that each word sounded precise and distinct, like pieces failing into predetermined places in some intricate pattern.

Peter Frankam's voice interrupted them. 'I was wondering how I'd manage to sit through the second half anyway. It's an ill wind and all that, eh?'

Dimitri introduced him to Mila, reluctantly. 'He's high up in Government. We were at Cambridge together once.'

Peter smiled affably, then turned to Helen. 'She was singing flat in the Schubert, wasn't she?'

'I don't know really. I wasn't listening properly.'

'It *was* rather tedious, wasn't it?'

Dimitri asked Mila if they could give her a lift home.

'No thank you. I live in Kowloon.'

'Not in the curfew area, I hope?'

'Near it.'

They talked about the curfew and the strike. Peter said it was hard to tell whether the management or the workers were being more unreasonable. Sleeking down his already well-groomed fair hair, he started assessing the trade union situation in Hong Kong.

It's like a news conference, Dimitri thought. He can't stop performing. He noticed Mila was smiling faintly as she listened. Her eyes met his for an instant and he thought he read the same mild derision in them that his own must have expressed.

'What do you think, though?' Peter turned to her suddenly, perhaps made uneasy by the silence of his audience. He changed to Cantonese. 'It takes a Chinese to understand the Chinese, after all ...'

But it was in her faultless, separated English that she answered him. 'Perhaps it is the beginning of the Cultural Revolution in Hong Kong?' she suggested.

XINHUA NEWS AGENCY

These atrocities are the result of long premeditation and are a component part of the British Government's scheme of collusion with U.S. imperialism against China. On the one hand in coordination with the U.S. imperialist war escalation in Vietnam, the British Government is continuing to provide the United States with Hong Kong as a base for aggression against Vietnam in disregard of the Chinese Government, and, on the other, it is steadily stepping up various hostile measures against China in Hong Kong ... The Hong Kong British authorities have turned loose large numbers of armed troops, policemen and riot police totalling more than 1000 on the bare-handed workers, representatives of various circles and young students, and have repeatedly attacked them with clubs, riot guns and tear-gas bombs, even turning out military vehicles and helicopters. Particularly since the unfolding of the great Proletarian Cultural Revolution in China, the British Authorities in Hong Kong have carried out repeated military and police manoeuvres hostile to China and aimed at the sanguinary suppression of Chinese residents in Hong Kong, vainly attempting to exclude the great influence of China's great Proletarian Cultural Revolution by high-handed tactics.

'Dimitri, Dimitri there's a picture of Jan in the paper !' Elena ran at him in her school clothes, waving the newspaper in her hand.

'With his tin hat on!' Alexander shouted from his room. '*I* was supposed to tell him anyway, you pig!'

'You were not!'

'I was! I saw it first!'

'You did not!' Her voice rose to a shriek, while Alexander's remained low and teasing.

'Pig.'

'Pig yourself!'

'Shut up both of you! Or I'll throw the bloody paper in the garbage.'

They checked themselves, then began to laugh.

'Yes and throw her with it,' Alexander giggled, pulling on his shoes. 'She smells like garbage anyway. Just right for a pig.'

Elena held her nose for reply as she swept past him.

Dimitri looked down at the newspaper. 'Who's driving you to school today, anyway?'

'The Normans.'

'Better hurry up, it's getting late.' He gazed at the large photograph beside the headline on the front page.

UGLY RIOTS IN KOWLOON. FIFTY-ONE ARRESTED

The photograph showed two Chinese policemen in steel helmets pushing a blood-stained demonstrator forward, his hands forced up behind his back so that he was bent double. One of the policemen seemed to be shouting at the man. The other was swinging his baton menacingly. The man had blood on his shirt. He looked small and weak. The policemen looked big and strong. In the background a European police officer was pointing up at a dimly lit building. It was Jan. He too looked large and strong, but older and stouter than the Chinese constables.

'Alexander, will you get a move on!' Helen's voice calling from the dining-room prevented Dimitri from reading the article. 'It's ten to eight! Elena's gone already!'

'Okay, okay.' Alexander wandered slowly out of his room to peer at the picture over Dimitri's arm. 'What's Jan doing?'

'Pointing.'

'Why?'

'Looks as though he's telling them where to shoot the tear gas.'

'Is he? Let's see. Maybe he'll get shot himself.'

'Hope not. We're going to a party of his next week.'

'Are you? Why?'

'He's retiring from the cops. Saying goodbye to all his pals.'

'You mean he's going to England?'

'Mm.'

'For God's sake, Dimitri, can't you tell him to get going?' Helen's voice again. 'The Normans are waiting downstairs and you have to start reading the paper with him!' She hurried down the hall in her kimono and chased Alexander out, hissing at Dimitri as she passed. 'Why must you *always* make everyone late? *Always!* You know how fussy the Normans are.'

'It's only eight minutes to. The Normans don't leave till five to.' Dimitri folded the paper and walked to the balcony to look down.

The Normans' brown Morris 1100 stood waiting eleven floors below. He saw Elena's long fair hair through the back window and then Alex jumping in. The door shut and the car moved off. He watched it turn the corner and then looked further away, across the steeply falling green hills to the sea, already burning bright under the morning sun. He narrowed his eyes against the glare. Far out towards Macau he could see the fishing fleet returning, a stream of little black dots with grey smudges of smoke staining the sky above them.

Helen was pouring the coffee. He looked down at the geranium pots along the edge of the balcony. The earth was cracked and dry. 'Did you water the plants last night?'

'No.'

'There's a picture of Jan in the paper.' He turned back to the table. 'Looks as though things are getting worse.'

She sighed, a little rueful sigh of resignation. 'How could things possibly get any worse?' Her voice had softened, the tenseness giving way to a tone of calmer but hopeless reproof. 'Why do you never help me get them off on time, Dimitri? I ask you so often.'

'Oh, just Russian slothfulness I suppose.' He sat down beside her. 'It's not really all that important, is it?'

The amah came in before Helen could answer, carrying a plate of burned toast.

'Ciosan, master.'

'Ciosan, Ah Wong.'

Ah Wong started clearing away the children's dishes, shaking her head at the mess they had left on the tablecloth. Her long pigtail hung down the back of her immaculate white tunic like a snake, the tip just flicking as she shook her head.

They started eating in their usual grey silence. Dimitri's eyes gazed absently across the room at the piano and the sheaves of music lying neat and undisturbed on top of it.

Can you play Edinburgh next Friday?

He looked down at his coffee and passed the newspaper wordlessly to Helen.

'Do you need the car this morning?' She laid the paper down after the briefest glance.

'I'll walk.'

'Will you be back for lunch?'

'No, I must get some work done on that article.'

He took his bamboo stick from the hall cupboard and left without saying goodbye. The lift was hot and airless. He switched on the fan and stood beneath it, turning his face up to the only slightly cooler draught from its whirring blades. On the fourth floor, Chan got in, neatly dressed in grey suit, sober tie and white shirt.

He bowed as he smiled at Dimitri. 'Good morning.'

"Morning.'

'It is very hot today.'

'Mm. Very.'

They stood watching the indicator register their descent, uncomfortably aware that they ought to find something to say.

'It seems to get hotter every day now.' Dimitri tapped the floor with his stick.

'Yes. But July and August are the worst months.'

'Yes, I suppose there's worse to come.'

Chan nodded at Dimitri's stick. 'You are going to walk?'

'Yes. This is my snake stick.'

'Oh. Be careful.'

The lift shuddered to a stop at the ground floor. The ceremony of leave-taking began as the doors slid open.

'After you.' Dimitri gestured.

'Please.'

'Go ahead.'

'Well, thank you.' Chan bowed slightly again as he left and walked to his brightly polished car.

Dimitri went the other way, feeling easier now that his encounter with Chan was over. Chan was a scientist who had become quite well known in his field. He had spent half his life in universities in England and America and now they had been neighbours for over five years. And yet their conversation never went beyond the rigid bounds of nervous small-talk. The mutual impenetrability of Chinese and Europeans in Hong Kong was nowhere denser than among the middle classes, he thought. Julie, a fisherman's daughter from a remote outlying island, felt no gap between east and west at all. Western education seemed to create, or at least widen, the gap rather than narrow it. Perhaps because it weakened confidence in the existing culture, the native self. That had not happened to Julie. She did not strain to live by another code than her own.

He climbed over the fence on to the hillside path that led to the university. Bamboo thickets, bushes and woods rose up above him to the Peak. Below, there was first the main road, then the steep terraced slopes which shelved down to the sea. The path itself was still in shade, the sun not yet far enough round to shine directly on to it. He walked quickly at first, but then more slowly as the silence and emptiness gradually took hold of him. Watching the patterned shadows of the leaves, he became quiet and empty too. This was the only time of the day when he felt securely alone and free.

He walked across the parapetless stone bridge before the Hospital. Two mangy brown dogs lay sprawled in front of him, sleeping. They knew him well and scarcely opened an eye as he stepped over them. Beneath the bridge nestled some squatter huts. A woman from the huts was washing clothes in a little stream of water, spreading them out on the bushes to dry. She glanced up at him with the same familiar casual indifference as her dogs. A transistor radio on a rock beside her was playing Western pop songs, sung in Cantonese.

The path was interrupted by the hospital buildings, tall grey blocks of concrete which yearly encroached on the scarred but resilient green. The clatter of pneumatic drills was never silenced here. He walked more quickly, the sun burning his back now that he was out of the shade. An ambulance and a police van drove slowly past him towards the casualty ward. The path began again a few steps later and he was among the trees once more. There was only the mortuary to pass now, an old building some way from the main hospital compound. After that there would be no more buildings until he reached the university two miles away.

The clashing of cymbals and gongs sounded far off through the trees, signal that a corpse was being taken from the mortuary for burial. Dimitri encountered a funeral nearly every time he walked along here and usually he stopped to watch. He walked on towards the sounds.

Now he could smell the scent of joss-sticks drifting heavily through the branches towards him. The seemingly aimless beating of gongs and chanting of prayers grew louder and more distinct. A woman's voice wailed. He reached the mortuary, which was just below the path, and looked down.

The squat grey building looked like a prison cell with its high, barred windows. It was wedged between the hill and the main road, which rose here to its highest point beside the path. A long barrel-shaped coffin had been taken out of the mortuary and placed on the pavement while the morning traffic snarled past two feet away. In front of the coffin, a large hearse was parked, its roof decked with flowers. A solemn photograph of the dead person, a forbidding woman of middle age, was set prominently in their midst. Round the coffin shuffled a Taoist priest in yellow and black robes, intoning prayers. The mourners, in white robes and headbands, stood or squatted on the pavement, watching stonily and occasionally chatting. The woman who had been wailing was very old, with grey hair and a gaunt face. She was keening quietly now, waving a lighted joss-stick mechanically in one hand. The funeral attendants, with that unconcern for the non-profitable which was the hallmark of Hong Kong, were sitting inside the hearse smoking and gossiping. They were paid to transport the coffin after all, not to fake sadness.

Dimitri turned and walked on. Death always checked him, put a stop in his thoughts. He recalled his father's grave, in the Japanese internment camp at Stanley Prison a quarter of a century ago. And his mother's in the cemetery at Happy Valley, only ten years away now. Earlier images, long sleeping, also awoke today. A Japanese soldier shooting a Chinese policeman before his bewildered and terrified nine-year-old eyes, and the headless stumps that had been British soldiers littering the Peak, decapitated after they had surrendered when their ammunition ran out. The thought of death, even natural death, had once for years absorbed him, abstracting him, as it chose to come, from conversations, books and even dreamless sleep. He used often to wake up at night possessed by thoughts of death as other men, in whom the sap of life flowed stronger, might have dwelled on images of women. Now that he was older, he was still captivated by these thoughts, but familiarity with them had bred, if not contempt, a half-resigned — an almost welcoming — acceptance.

He walked on into the trees, holding his stick tighter. The long grass beside the path was thickest here and he had seen a cobra twice already slipping across the grey stones only a foot or two in front of him. While he stepped gingerly forward, he thought of Jan again. Jan had been beside him at all the deaths he had seen, his father's, his mother's, the battlefield on the Peak, even that casual shooting of the Chinese constable by the first Japanese soldier Dimitri ever saw. He could feel even now the rough comforting palm of Jan's hand pulling his head away from the sight of the blood spluttering and bubbling out of the dying man's mouth. The same hand had gripped his shoulder at Stanley in front of the bamboo cross on the bare little mound which covered his father. Perhaps — he could not remember now — it had held his arm too at the later funeral of his mother. Now that Jan was retiring, leaving Hong Kong, almost the last visible thread that tied Dimitri to his childhood and youth would be snapped. That's middle age, he thought, not bitterly, but with a rueful acquiescence.

He turned a corner and stopped short. The cobra lay coiled on the path six feet away and over it stood Frank Browning, stirring it gently with a broken branch.

'Hello, Dimitri. Good morning.' Frank glanced up at him and then returned to work.

'Frank, that's a cobra.'

'Yes.' He was running the stick along its back, absorbed apparently in the way the smooth skin rippled.

Suddenly the snake lifted its head. Its hood puffed out and its forked tongue flickered rapidly.

'Now you've scared it.' Frank stepped back and looked at Dimitri reproachfully. He threw the branch away, took off his glasses and started polishing them on his shirt.

The cobra's head swayed, hissing menacingly for some seconds, then sank down. Dimitri realised that his heart was thumping rapidly. The snake slid away into the grass, the tip of its tail still lying on the path and flicking angrily.

'If I picked him up by his tail and held him at arm's length, he wouldn't be able to bite me.'

Dimitri stepped past cautiously. 'Haven't you done enough?' His voice was unsteady.

'He likes me. We've met before.'

'Have you poked it like that before?'

Frank put his glasses back on. 'I wasn't poking, I was tickling.'

Dimitri kept glancing back over his shoulder as they walked along. His heart was still pounding faintly, high in his chest. 'Either you know a lot about snakes, or else you're as mad as a hatter.'

'Oh it's all a matter of confidence. Like lion-tamers, you know. I whisper to them. It keeps them calm.' He was beginning to puff, his round short legs unable to keep pace with Dimitri. 'Do go a bit slower.'

Dimitri slackened his steps. They walked on, as they usually did, in silence. They seldom met on the path, Frank being an early riser, but even when they did, they rarely talked, preferring an amiable ruminative silence, which was interrupted only by the jingles Frank occasionally hummed to himself. In any case, Frank would leave the path soon, scrambling down the hillside to the road where his laboratory stood.

While Frank did not divert Dimitri's thoughts from death, he did give them a different tone. Frank cultivated a self-conscious eccentricity which often manifested itself as a hectoring optimism in face of everything. A fresher memory recurred. A middle-aged lecturer in psychology, Jack Tingall, having just learned he had cancer, leaning on the bar as he tearfully reckoned his prospects of survival. An embarrassed, withdrawing silence all round him. Then Frank's blithe injunction slicing through the maudlin haze, 'Go and exercise your gonads in the Suzy Wong strip old chap, while you've still got the chance.' Frank's sympathetic warmth could carry bluffness like this off, whereas the same words from colder men, such as Dimitri himself, could only have been cruel.

'What happened to Jack Tingall?' Dimitri asked suddenly. 'He resigned, didn't he? Did he get cured?'

'Died. Fifty good years, can't complain.'

Dimitri shrugged. They walked on silently for several minutes. Frank hummed an unrecognisable tune. Dimitri watched a hawk circling high above them, its ragged wings scarcely moving. It seemed impossible that they were only half an hour away from the two million people of Victoria and Kowloon. As the hawk circled endlessly, his thoughts went round too, round and round his marriage with Helen, another form, it seemed, of death. In baffled remorse he followed a tangled maze of memories, complaints and excuses, that brought him always back to the same place.

There had always been, he realised now, a quickness about her movements, a slightly frantic touch to everything she did, that he had not noticed, or had not understood, from the very beginning. The nervousness of a creature constantly alert, anxious, fearful of attack. The tears and depressions when the critiques of her concerts were slighting, the relentless hours of practice, impatience of rest, of vacancy, even of the essential indolence of love — all these, he now recognised with painful surprise, all these had been the qualities that had first drawn him to her. They were the sharp edges of a being that he had later found difficult, and now at last unbearable, to touch. Life seemed to consist for her of an unending series of confrontations and crises that could be handled and surmounted only with the utmost hardship and disturbance. When the events in themselves had been considerable, when they had concerned the rise and fall of her musical career, it had been bad enough. But now that they were the trivia of daily life, it was unendurable. Getting the children off to school, for instance, seemed to exhaust her of as much nervous energy as the preparation for her first professional concert. She ran, rather than walked, through the flat, shouting at both of them, excitedly reminding them of every minute that passed, leaving her food half-eaten, her coffee half-drunk, her cup half off the saucer. Every day occurred some heart-stopping scene because Alexander had left one of his books behind, or his packed lunch, or Elena had not taken her vitamin pill. Such nervous intensity, spent on such trifles seemed to Dimitri's cool, phlegmatic temperament to be a sort of madness. It had pulled them apart and left jagged edges.

Can you play Edinburgh next Friday?

Memories. Of her moodiness before a concert. Of breathlessness. Of sudden fits of fears and self-doubt. Of tempests over a loose shoe buckle or a missing button. Of her always draining dependence on his being there, being in *this* seat, not *that*, sometimes even for repeat performances of the same programme in the same week…

A self-induced delusion of eventual success and recognition had buoyed them both then, and he had been able to accept, even enjoy perhaps, all that frenetic intensity, in the deceptive assurance that it was productive. He was sure, then, that she was a great pianist, and that, once established, she would be able to let go, to live securely and serenely upon the plateau she would have precariously reached after so much hectic toil. But now -

Memories again. Of hours away from his thesis on Russian literature to hear her practise, although he was musically uneducated. Of letters to agents composed and recomposed and finally torn up. Of sudden groundless fears for her hands and panicky visits to doctors and specialists and yet more specialists. Of the thick gloves she wore before concerts, even in summer, as a precaution against shutting her fingers in a door…

How was it that he had accepted, or participated, in all this then, while now even the mere remembrance of it roused a tremor of irritation in his throat? What had vanished now was not just the empty hopes of success, but also the illusory mists of love that had protected everything she did from his normally bleak, investigating eye. The mists had dissolved in the increasing nervousness that fewer engagements and harsher critiques, the sense of bitterness and failure, had inevitably produced. When finally she had given up hopes of a performing career, she had, almost in revenge, deserted the piano altogether. She would not play as an amateur, or give lessons — that was too painful a reminder of broken hopes — so all her violent energy had been channelled on to the children and himself, a torrent of anxious caring which nearly overwhelmed them but did not really satisfy her. He recalled the long hours she used to spend devotedly, too devotedly, on criticism of his early papers although she knew no Russian. When he had weaned her from that, there seemed nothing left at all for her except perpetual child-care and recurrent despair.

I should have foreseen all this, he thought. We shouldn't have married, shouldn't have had children. I should have known it was *her*, not her career, that made her such a fireball of moody self-destructive energy. Somewhere in her cells the code was written and nothing can erase it now.

And yet there were other memories too. Of her room in London when he had come in quietly without her knowing and listened to her playing Brahms. She gave the cascades of sound a softness then like shafts of sunlight slanting through closed curtains, a softness that was mellow and richly varied, always trembling and fading. That's good, he had known then, that's good, And he had never heard a piano sing like that again. Her body too, then, her long wavy hair, was moulded into curves, echoing the music it seemed, expressing it as much as her hands and feet. There was no part of her that was not playing, no part that had not lost its tense angularity and become as fluid and tranquil as the music. It's the music that's playing her, he had thought then, not her the music.

He turned to Frank suddenly and asked in an assumed bantering tone. 'What makes so many women unhappy in marriage?'

'Mm? Not enough screwing.' Frank took off his glasses, which had misted over again, and wiped them as he walked. 'Hubby goes to work, meets people, has interests and so on, while the little woman, just as smart as he is, I dare say, has to stay behind brooding in the nest. She'd like to be out doing something too, but she can't. At least, not without neglecting the brood, which only makes her feel guilty, and then she's even worse off. Only solution is to take their minds off it, and screw them silly. Most men don't do enough of that. Makes them both happy, matter of fact. Discharge of energy, you know. Your human being's nothing more than a bunch of particles with positive and negative charges after all. That's why I took a job out here in the tropics, so's I could stay randy longer.'

Dimitri laughed. 'Your *simplisme* is charming, but hardly meets the case.'

'Your case?'

'*The* case.'

'Well, there you are, take it or leave it. Can't do better than that. Can you?'

'No.'

Frank's words had cut deeper than his belittlement of them suggested. Helen had resisted love for two years or more now. Since the birth of Elena, they had rarely slept together anyway, but now she avoided him altogether. It was because of her refusals that he had begun to desire her less and other women more. An unsatisfied lust, or randiness as Frank would have called it, and also a simple need for self-forgetfulness, had combined to send him searching for bar-girls. From them he found he could buy a few hours' warm obliviousness as well as the pleasures Helen had denied him, or perhaps had never had it in her power to give.

'I see the rioters are out again,' Frank interrupted his brooding. 'All of us foreign devils may be thrown out of here before long.'

'I suppose that depends on what Peking wants. Would you be sorry to leave, though?'

'I'd be sorry to leave with a bayonet in my back, I can tell you that.'

'No doubt you'd find another tropical setting where your randiness could flourish.'

'Well, I'd try, mate, you can be sure of that. Of course you were born here, weren't you?'

'Mm.'

'I suppose you could apply to Chairman Mao to be left in your homeland undisturbed in that case. How would that appeal to you?'

'Not particularly.'

'You might become a *cause célèbre*.'

Dimitri only grunted. They walked the rest of the way without speaking, until Frank turned off to the main road.

'Well Dimitri, thank you for your company. Been a pleasure to walk with such a cultivated man as yourself, even if our communion was mostly wordless. I bid you farewell.' He slithered away through the bushes, cracking the twigs and sending little avalanches of stones before him.

Dimitri wondered as he walked on alone how much of Frank's bland, optimistic facade could be more than a facade, a mask which despite constant wearing had failed to shape the face beneath. Surely when he was alone he could not think and act like that? His was a public style that demanded an audience. In an empty theatre it would sound hollow and false. He thought of Frank's second wife — the first had left him five years ago — a young but aloof woman who was rarely seen together with him. The three children of his earlier marriage were sullen and distant too, as if they resented not only their stepmother but the rest of the world as well. Frank's recipe for a happy marriage either did not seem to work in his own case or else had not even been tried.

The path started winding down round the shoulder of the hill and the sunlit harbour opened out below him, with the encircling hills of Kowloon already hazed in heat behind it. An American aircraft-carrier from Vietnam lay at anchor in the middle of the harbour, its massive dark grey bulk dominating the blue waters. A number of sleek destroyers were berthed around her, but they were lost almost at once among the hundred or so merchant ships that lay scattered nearby, discharging cargo into lighters packed against their sides. Two junks with patched, faded sails seemed almost motionless as they beat towards the typhoon shelter, looking from the hillside like toy boats on a placid pond. A P&O liner, gleaming white with yellow stacks, was slipping from its berth at the Ocean Terminal. The sight of it released yet another long-submerged memory in Dimitri.

Walking with Helen in London one summer Sunday morning, walking across Tower Bridge and pausing to watch another P&O boat putting out to sea. They had walked all morning through the city, deserted of traffic and workers, and eaten scrambled eggs in a sailors' restaurant by the docks. Then, for a time, there had been warmth and quiet between them. Then she had seemed to be rising and agents wanted her. Perhaps if that had only gone right, the warmth and peace would still be there.

Out of the shade now, he felt the sun scorching his back again. The red and green roofs of the university spread out amongst the trees beneath him, tall, still palms rising from the azalea bushes and magnolias. He could see the main road further down, wriggling between the high blocks of Sai Ying Pun like a glittering black snake. Halfway down the hill, he passed the green iron pavilion which looked out over the sea to Lantau, Island. The old Chinese man and his wife were there as usual, performing the involved gestures of Tai Chi. The man's wrinkled face smiled as Dimitri passed. He was poised on one foot, moving his arms in slow, intent gestures. His wife stood motionless on widespread feet, arms outstretched, moving only her head. Hanging from the roof was a bamboo bird cage covered with a cloth, from which a low, quiet cheeping came.

'Ciosan,' Dimitri nodded.

The man paused. 'Ciosan. Very hot, uh?'

"Hai, ho yi.'

'Always walking, walking uh?' And he resumed his stance.

The air seemed to grow more humid as Dimitri went down the hill. He was sweating heavily now.

The air-conditioner was vibrating noisily in his room, but he was grateful for its reviving flow of cool dry air. He slumped into his chair. On the desk before him lay a stencilled notice.

> *Owing to the strike of public transport workers, examinations scheduled for today have been postponed. New dates and times will be announced in due course.*

On the corner of the notice his secretary had written: *Please phone Mrs Johnston at home.*

He gazed at the notice for some seconds before dropping it in the wastepaper basket, remembering Frank Browning's pink-cheeked face. I'd be sorry to leave with a bayonet in my back.

He picked up the phone. Helen left messages like this several times a week, often only to reiterate something she had said at breakfast or to ask his advice on some simple domestic matter, like whether she should give the children fish or meat for dinner. No amount of exaggerated indifference to these questions could make her stop asking them.

'Ah Wong, is missy there?'

'Missy go out.'

He changed to Cantonese. 'Did she say when she was coming back?'

'No. She took the car.' Ah Wong sounded bad-tempered. Her voice had become flat and sullen. 'Radio says no more buses. I told her no buses, she took the car.'

'All right. Thank you.'

He leant back, considering. Helen was too anxious to stray into the riot area, but it was strange that she had gone out at all. Yet it was like her to have phoned and then left at once without waiting for his call. Probably it was some trivial piece of shopping she wanted to consult him about. He gazed round his room. His books looked stolidly back at him from the shelves lining the walls. A reproduction of a sketch by Ni Tsan hung down on its rather faded scroll. Near the window hung another scroll, a mannered quotation from Confucius, done by a student, in uneven strokes, several years ago. He read it through for the hundredth vacant time and wondered why he still kept it there.

> Students of old fixed their eyes upon themselves: now
> they learn with their eyes upon others.

The student who had given it to him had been a small phthisic girl, with white hands along which her blue veins ramified in unhealthy clarity. She had gone to America, after months of anxious waiting for a visa, and he had never heard from her since. She was one of the few who had succeeded in escaping the uncertainties of the eventual re-absorption of Hong Kong into China, which sometime in their lifetime would inevitably come. And perhaps sooner rather than later, he thought, glancing out of the window at the stone courtyard and the branches of the magnolia tree overspreading the little pond. Above and behind its thick green leaves, the top of the clock tower jutted up from the great hall, a strangely harmonious combination of Gothic red-brick and vaguely Eastern architecture.

He opened the top drawer of his desk and took out the article he was writing. Having left it for over a week, he could scarcely recall more than the general plan of the argument. One of his pleasures was this rediscovery of thought that occurred when he returned to something he had been working on and left for some time. Being self-mistrustful, he always expected a re-reading to be disillusioning, and so was always surprised and pleased whenever he found that what he had written was not entirely mediocre.

Fastened to the top page with a rusty paper clip was a cutting he had torn out of *The Times*, an advertisement for a post in London. The closing date was next week. Perhaps sooner rather than later, he thought again. Perhaps the old Chinese landlord was ready now to repossess the once barren tenement that had become so populous and so profitable. If he was, it would not be done without some throat-cutting. He remembered last year's riots, when some Europeans were burned alive in their cars, and decided to draft an application, not quite sure whether he was serious or not.

The Chinese art of gardening, more earthy than the Japanese, had been well applied to the university grounds. Part garden, part unplanned woods and shrubs, the grounds dropped down from the library in broken steps and slopes crossed by winding, shaded paths. Dimitri was taking his application to the post office. There were few students about, most of them staying at home because of the transport strike, but some were strolling on the grass, broken by rocks and hillocks, round the lily pond. A Japanese would have raked and cultivated this, modelling even the roots of the trees, and an Englishman would have smoothed it into an Oxbridge quad. He preferred the Chinese attitude, which left the earth alone when it was not to be used for crops and profit.

A girl from his first-year class smiled at him. She was pretty and slim, in the briefest of dresses, which revealed her slender legs like a ballet skirt. He thought of Voltaire's description of Mme de Chatelet's legs — 'the twin glories of France'. 'The twin glories of Hong Kong' would hardly do, although this girl's were almost certainly more glorious that Mme de Chatelet's could ever have been. She was walking hand in hand with a boy and he heard them laugh. He felt a little ridiculous, carrying the letter in his hand, when he contrasted the twinge of apprehension that had led him to write it with the apparent unconcern of these two young students. But he recalled the broadcast he had listened to from Peking last night, with its vague yet heavy menace, and walked on re-determined.

Near the main road, he saw C. K. Tsong in front of him. C.K. was a small, wizened scholar with that appearance of sagacity which age often imparts to a wrinkled face with heavy lids and sharp brown eyes. He walked erect and neat despite the torture he had suffered as a prisoner of the Japanese, which had left scars on his wrists and legs. Dimitri's long strides soon overtook him. C.K. smiled briefly and they went along together.

They walked some steps in silence until Dimitri asked a self-consciously perfunctory question. 'What do you make of all these riots, C.K.?'

He smiled, with a wintry sort of warmth. 'It is a spillover from the mainland. They have a cultural revolution on the mainland, so it is only patriotic to have one here too.'

'Yes, I suppose so. Will it get worse, do you think?'

'If they want it to. It is nothing compared with what has happened already in China ... My brother is still in Shanghai, you know.'

'Is he?'

'He knows that pianist well.'

'The one who is supposed to have had his fingers broken by the Red Guards?'

'For playing bourgeois music, yes.' C.K. spoke about the pianist's rumoured maiming in that quiet matter-of-fact manner which the Chinese seemed always to adopt towards the outrages that human beings committed on each other. It did not mean a lack of pity; rather a sense of the futility of protest. Oppression and cruelty were for them as inevitable a part of human life as typhoons, floods and famines. 'I am sure he would still prefer to be in China,' C.K. went on, calmly.

'Your brother?,

'The pianist.' He stopped at the steps of the Fung Ping Shan museum. 'If I had stayed in Shanghai and never been to America, I would never have left, not even now, in this so-called Cultural Revolution.'

'You might not have been allowed to leave now.'

'There is always a way. But now I am half-Westernised. Like most people in Hong Kong. They do not think we are proper Chinese any more, in China. Neither one thing nor the other. Not fish nor fowl, you say?'

'Why not both, then?' Dimitri shrugged, half jocularly.

But C.K. shook his head doggedly. 'Not for us. One thing or the other is best.' He bowed his head and walked up the steps, slight, erect and, as ever, forbidding.

His mind is always made up, like a book that's already written, Dimitri thought as he went on. He doesn't discuss with you, be reads from his inner book.

The sun was at its zenith now. There was no shade from its fierceness, even in the narrow street he was walking along with its tall, bare, concrete apartment blocks. The midday traffic rumbled and whined past, hardly any the less, it seemed, for the absence of the striking buses. Lorries and vans were stopping everywhere to pick up unofficial passengers. Dimitri read the notice on one which asked for twice the normal bus fare. Working class solidarity, the brotherhood of the proletarian masses.

After a time, the road curved sharply down towards the older part of town, where occasional decaying houses with crumbling stone balustrades, relics of a more leisurely age, were insecurely wedged between the new high-rise living slots. These few old buildings lived out their last years, like impoverished, aged gentlefolk, in precarious and fading dignity. The expiry of a lease, the death of an owner, and the new order would move in with the omnivorous bulldozer and crane. Every hundred yards or so, something was being torn down and rebuilt. The flaking masonry crashed in a cloud of ashen powdery dust and was carted away in overloaded lorries belching diesel smoke from broken exhausts. He tried to remember what this street had looked like fifteen years ago, when he had come back from Cambridge. There used to be a large, quiet house, standing back in a tree-lined garden, a house that had always kept its windows shuttered.

The pit-pat of hawkers' sandals and their hoarse, repeated cries as they jogged along with that lilting trot that balanced their swaying bamboo poles across their shoulders. Their sweaty, sunburned, rivelled faces peering up at the upper windows where amahs would lean out and bargain before condescending to come down and buy. And the rickshaw boys, lean men with bulging calves and stringy veins, smoking in the shade of their canopies or loping along, panting and sweating, while fat women with shopping bags sat inside and watched their human draught animals with supercilious indifference.

He realised he was passing a block of flats now where the old cobbler used to work, a gaunt white-haired old man with round, rimless glasses halfway down his nose and a straggling mandarin beard. Dimitri always used to take his shoes there to be mended. The old man, dressed in traditional black, would peer first up at his face, then down at the shoes, and then hang them on a nail on the little wooden stall which he set up every day against the wall. When Dimitri came back, the old man would peer up at his face again and then reach unerringly for the right shoes from amongst twenty or thirty pairs. He never talked except to name his price, and Dimitri never bargained since his price was always so low. For years, whenever he passed, be had seen the old man there, bent over his work, glasses halfway down his nose, a strip of leather on his lap. Then one day he was gone. The bulldozers were crushing the wall and levelling the ground behind it and the block of flats he was passing now, already itself flaking and tatty, had gone up, graceless and inhuman. He had never seen the cobbler again. Now his shoes went to a shop which issued tickets with small-print cautions and a blue-stamped collection date.

It was, paradoxically, the communist revolution in China that had changed Hong Kong from dozy backwater to capitalist boomtown. Every capitalist in China that had not been killed or imprisoned, and every would-be capitalist, had been filtered through the years into Hong Kong. Like through a drainage system, he thought. And every one of them worshipped the golden calf with brutal enthusiasm, hoping only for enough time to fill a foreign bank account before the communists at last swept over the Kowloon hills and in their own no less brutal style stamped out the cult and replaced it with their own.

Perhaps sooner rather than later, he thought once more, glancing down at the blue airmail letter in his hand. Grey-white dust from a building site drifted across the street in front of him and the narrow pavement was blocked by a crowd of people at the bus stop, fighting to climb on to a lorry that had pulled in to pick them up. The post office was across the road. He paused on the kerb, waiting for a chance to slip across through a gap in the traffic. Sweat was trickling down his face and arms and his shirt felt wet where it clung to his body. As he stood there waiting, he saw Helen driving round the corner and up the street towards him. For a moment he hesitated, then stepped back so that she wouldn't notice him. She drove past, her eyes shielded by the dark sunglasses she always wore, her lips tight and down-set at the corners. She seemed to be frowning, sitting slightly hunched over the wheel.

She was gone. But he stood on the kerb, still gazing blankly at the traffic blurring past after her, while his eyes still held the image of that taut, unhappy face. Everything about her is so tight and compressed, he thought sadly, and then, How can we go on if I want to avoid her like that?

A break came at last in the rush of traffic and he dodged across the road.

He came home in the evening on an open lorry packed to the tailboard with fisherwomen from Aberdeen. The driver charged him a dollar, instead of the normal bus fare of thirty cents, and the women stared at him with a kind of dull, neutral curiosity. Only when they heard him speaking Cantonese to the driver, did their eyes quicken slightly and some nudged each other and giggled, as if it was absurd, yet commendable, for a foreign devil to try to speak their language.

As he jumped off at the approach to the university flats, a convoy of police trucks drove past the other way, sirens screaming continuously. He counted six of them, each lined with steel-helmeted policemen carrying rifles and gas-masks. Perhaps sooner rather than later, he thought once again. They're not joking.

He walked up the steep, winding road, the evening sun still fierce on his back. The kapok tree at the top was in bloom, mysteriously weightless fleecy puffs, floating, apparently, on the bare branches. He remembered when it was small and fragile, bearing only two or three blossoms a year. That was when Elena had been born and he had come back from the hospital and stood by the tree in the dusk, whispering Oh God, not another child. Not another.

He looked up at his flat on the eleventh floor. Helen was leaning over the balcony, looking down at him. For some seconds they looked at each other as he walked along, and then she turned and went in, without acknowledging him. Each of them was avoiding the other.

'Hallo, Dimitri, did you have a nice day?'
'Hallo, Elena.'
'Did you have a nice day?'
'A day of memories...'
'A day of what? Oh yes, did you know there's a curfew tonight, right here? We can't go out after eleven. It's on the radio. It's the first curfew since the Japanese war, they said, the first actually on Hong Kong island ... Of course, there've been lots in Kowloon. Dimitri, why do they call it a curfew? Did you see all those police trucks? Where were they going? When was the Japanese war, Dimitri? Was it years and years ago or not very long?'

When the children are grown up I'll go away. I don't want to play the piano any more. I don't want to do anything except to go away. Go away from everything and everyone.

It's all so grey now. Nothing but trivial job after trivial job. I wake up at night and I can't sleep any more and I look out of the window at the sky and I wish I could go as far away as the stars. Because I don't belong here. I don't belong anywhere any more. Once I really wanted to play, to play well, but now I don't care about it at all.

Dimitri hates me, I know he does. Only he doesn't say so. I catch him looking at me and he's hating me because I'm so depressed and nervous all the time. And I don't even make love with him any more. I can't. I don't like it any more. It's for people who are happy with each other.

Yes, only the children need me, and that will only be for a few years now. Then there'll be no-one, nothing. I know I hate looking after them, but it's the only point left to my life now.

Look at the lines growing into my face. Furrows, trenches.

He doesn't realise what it's like to have wanted something so much and worked so hard on it and given up so much for it, and then see it all just slipping out of your hand after all. My mother worked as a typist for years, to pay for my lessons. But it's all wasted now. Better if I'd never had a lesson in my life. He doesn't know what it's like to feel that bitterness rising up your throat all the time. Because something might have come of me with a bit more luck. There was a time when I was good, I know I was good. But it didn't work out. He doesn't understand what it's like to drag yourself through every day, working at house and children and shopping and homework when all the time all you really want to do is let go and cry. He can't understand that.

Sometimes I think I'm selfish. I just sit and brood about myself. I don't even read the newspapers. Perhaps I'd feel different if I did something for other people. But I just don't care about them enough. And anyway, if I did do something, it would only be to take my mind off myself, not to help them. No, there's only one thing I ever cared about and now that's gone.

Can you play Edinburgh next Friday? I think that was it, that's what finally broke me. If only it had come a week or two earlier, I might still have come to something. People might have heard of me. But after that, I just couldn't pick myself up. Not again, not any more. And there was nothing else to fall back on, nothing else I'd ever wanted to do. But I wanted that, I wanted that so very much. It's strange, because

I feel so empty and cold towards it now, as if it couldn't have been me. But it was me. It was, it was.

The tram was still smouldering on the waterfront, oily black smoke drifting away from its charred framework into the dark of the harbour. Round it stood a squad of riot police, looking up at the old tenement buildings where longshoremen, coolies and prostitutes lived. Some of the policemen held rifles on their hips, fingers crooked round the triggers. A police Landrover's headlights were glaring over the wreckage, its red roof-light calmly revolving. The road was littered with jagged jewels of glass, glittering like cat's eyes in the gleam of the lights.

A policeman waved Dimitri past. He heard a radio crackling in the back of the Landrover, smelt the bitter smell of burnt rubber and felt the crunch of glass under his tyres.

'What's it like further on?' he asked in Cantonese.

'Better go the other way. They're out for foreign devils tonight.'

The noise of chattering and laughing sounded muffled through the heavy teak door of Jan's apartment on the Peak. Jan opened the door himself. The lights were bright, the room full of people talking, laughing, drinking and nibbling.

'Dimitri!' Jan hugged him in his usual embrace. 'I was afraid you weren't coming. Where's Helen?'

'Headache. She's sorry she couldn't make it — she'll make the next one all right.' He spied Peter Frankam across the room talking to Elena's ballet teacher. Several of the dwindling band of Jan's Russian *émigré* friends stood by the window, grey-haired, lined, but unsubdued.

'I nearly didn't get here, by the way.' He looked back at Jan. 'There was a tram burnt out in Connaught Road and the cops sent me the long way round.'

'Ach never mind, you got here after all.' Jan's eyes looked small and tired. He was swaying slightly, his arm still affectionately round Dimitri's shoulder. 'All these people are the doll wonns. Tell Helen not to miss the next party. These are the wonns I have to ask, the next wonn will be only people I like.'

'Do I come in both categories then, Jan?'

'Ah?' But someone was calling him across the room. He squeezed Dimitri's shoulder again and turned away.

Dimitri edged his way between the groups of people. Nearly everyone he met was a government servant, in the Police or Legal Department. He saw Lisa talking by the sideboard to Reuben Sternor, an old Russian Jew from Shanghai. Now he was bald and wrinkled, but once, as Dimitri fadedly remembered, he had been dapper and vigorous, a dealer in radios and cameras, who used to visit his mother frequently in the early years after the war. Lisa too looked tired, her light blue Russian eyes lack-lustre now. Her hair was grey and her face had the pallor of someone who never went into the sun, as if she had not wanted to lose even the slightest trace of her Moscow origin.

'Well, Lisa.' He poured himself some vodka. The sideboard had not changed for twenty years, an ugly, government-issue lump of varnished teak. 'Are you sorry to be going at last?'

'Jan will be sorry.' She never disclosed her own feelings, a certain abruptness whenever they were sounded showing that nearer approach was unwelcome.

Reuben smiled at him, his brown eyes half-lidded. 'Perhaps, if these troubles go on, we shall all be leaving together. A lot of people are moving their money out ... I need a drink, excuse me.'

Dimitri thought of his application to London and smiled too. Everyone was looking for a bolt hole. But he said nothing, feeling obscurely ashamed to acknowledge that he too was apprehensive.

'This is the first night Jan has had off in three weeks,' Lisa was saying. 'They are trying to wear the police down till the government has to call in troops, and then what will Peking do?'

Dimitri evaded that question. 'But Jan will never be happy in a cottage in England. He will have to do something.'

'He's dreading it, Dimitri.' Lisa suddenly laid her hand on his wrist. 'He's dreading it. It's like cutting his arm off.'

Dimitri followed her anxious glance across the room. Jan was talking to Peter Frankam now, rocking back on his heels, arms outspread, his laugh boisterously loud. Peter was smoothing his eyebrows with his middle finger and smiling politely — trying to advertise, surely, both boredom and condescension.

'Is Helen here?'

'No, Lisa.'

'Oh.'

'She had one of her headaches. She was sorry to miss it.'

Dimitri swallowed his vodka quickly and poured some more. He felt Lisa watching him. 'What does Jan see in Peter Frankam?'

'Are you happy Dimitri?'

Dimitri looked across the room at Jan again. 'Wer ist gluecklich in der Welt?'

'Because you're drinking rather fast. You know I don't understand German.'

'Lisa, you wouldn't let anyone ask you that question. Why do you think I'm going to let anyone ask me?'

'You always escape.,

'You always forbid. We're the same, at bottom.'

She smiled, raising her eyebrows reflectively. Reuben was back with a glass of white wine. Lisa's eyes watched reproachfully as Dimitri moved away, taking the vodka bottle with him.

'Where's Helen, Dimitri?' Peter Frankam caught him on the way to the verandah.

'Headache.'

'Pity. I wanted her advice on a recording I was thinking of getting.'

'Why don't you ring her up?'

'Pierre Boulez,' Peter was not going to miss the chance of cultural display to an audience of hard-nosed lawyers and police officers. 'It has rather closer affinities to the Javanese than usual.'

'Ring her up, Peter. It's no good telling me, I'm practically tone-deaf.'

'Oh I know that's not true ... We must get together soon, though, Dimitri. It's terrible how one only meets one's friends at other people's parties ...' He took a handkerchief out of his breast pocket, dabbed his forehead and replaced it carefully. Everyone else was in shirt sleeves, but Peter, characteristically, wore a jacket and tie.

The verandah overlooked the slopes of Pokfulam and the sea beyond. Dimitri lay back in a cane chair, his feet among the carefully tended cactuses that Lisa would soon have to leave behind, and gazed at the light of the sinking moon, slanting in a widening, silver gleam across the leaden sea.

It was strange that Lisa had touched his arm like that. Jan had always hugged and embraced him exuberantly, but he could not remember Lisa ever touching him before. Not even in the Japanese internment camp at Stanley, or, years later, when she met him at the airport to tell him his mother was dying.

'How is she, Lisa.?'

'She's going, Dimitri. We have to hurry.'

The blurred taxi ride through the grim, sunless February morning. His mother's waxen face on the not too clean pillow.

'Is your child born yet?' she'd muttered huskily in Russian, her breath hot and dry.

'Two days ago.'

'Boy or girl?'

'Boy.'

'What colour is his hair?'

Half an hour later she was dead.

'She was holding on to hear,' Lisa had said simply. 'She wanted to know before she died.'

But Lisa then was erect and calm. The hand she had laid on his arm just now was the first gesture of uncertainty or appeal he had ever seen her make. She had always been utterly self-possessed, even in the internment camp.

His mother waving the flies off his father's dying face, sponging his burning forehead with a strip of rag, and murmuring all the time with Lisa, reciting the names of unknown Russian and Chinese towns. The liquid syllables flowing in the dark heat of the hut like some religious chant, each name calling forth a nod, a smile, of sad, proud recognition in the endlessly celebrated communion of exile. Not even then, not even after she had covered his father's bony face with the rag, gently taken from his mother's heedless fingers, not even then had Lisa ever touched him to give or ask for comfort.

He became aware of someone else, on the far corner of the verandah. He saw in the dark that it was Elena's ballet teacher, leaning over the railing.

She had noticed him too. 'I am sorry. Do I disturb you?'

He remembered the precise separateness of her words when they met before. He held up his glass to examine it. 'You ought to know better than to interrupt a man at his reveries.' She turned her face away, looking out towards the sea.

'In case you're offended,' Dimitri swished the vodka round and round in his glass, 'I was joking when I said that.'

Her shoulders seemed to lift faintly, but she did not answer. She was wearing a long dress, cut low at the back. He could make out the rippling movement of her shoulder blades as she shrugged.

'Are you offended?'

'You ought to know better than to interrupt a woman at her reveries.' She laughed, A high-pitched tinkling laugh. Only Julie's laugh, of all the Chinese girls he had known, was low and husky.

He bowed his head in acknowledgement of her riposte. 'I'm sorry, I've forgotten your name. We've met before, you remember.'

'Yes, at the City Hall. You are Elena's father.'

'And you are?'

'Mila Chan.'

'Mila, that's right. I saw you dancing on TV the other night.'

'Did you?' She turned to face him now, leaning back against the railing so that light from the room fell on her face. 'Did you like it?'

'I'm a poor judge. Dancing's never appealed to me much.'

She looked at him with serious eyes, but faintly smiling lips, as if she were considering another retort. But she only asked, 'Is Mrs Johnston here?'

'Headache.'

'Oh.'

'Diplomatic. She doesn't like parties.'

She looked at him still with the same grave eyes and the same smile flickering uncertainly round her lips.

'She doesn't like anything much.' He lifted the vodka bottle from the tiled floor beside the chair and emptied it into his glass. 'Do you?'

'Do I?'

'Do you like anything much?'

The almost imperceptible shrug again. 'I like dancing.'

'Is Elena any good at it? Because if she shows the slightest promise I think I'll stop her lessons at once.'

Her eyebrows lifted slightly. He noticed how finely they curved. She was waiting for him to explain.

'I don't want her to go through the same as — to aspire beyond what's possible, I mean ...' He gazed down at his glass meditatively, 'The same as my wife, I was going to say, of course. As you no doubt realise.' He drank, looking past Mila at the sea again. The lights of the fishing fleet from Aberdeen were clustered close together, near the dim line of the horizon. 'Did you know she started as a concert pianist?'

'No?'

'Well, never mind,' switching his eyes back to Mila. 'What about you, what did you start as?'

The door opened behind him. The noise of chatter and laughter suddenly rose and then fell again as the door was closed. They had both paused and waited, as if hoping they would not be disturbed.

'What did you start as?' he asked again.

'I started as a baby in Shanghai.'

'So did eleven million others. When did you come to Hong Kong?'

'About a year ago this time. I come and go.'

'Why?'

She put her head on one side, frowning. 'Many reasons.'

'Meaning I shouldn't ask impertinent questions.' He got up and leant beside her on the railing, she still looking back into the room, he out over the sea. 'Well, now it's your turn. You ask me some.'

'How long have you been in Hong Kong?' She laughed her delicate tinkling laugh again. 'Is that impertinent?'

'I was born here.'

'Ah. So you are an old China Coast bum.'

He snorted. 'That's impertinent, anyway. I may be a bum and I may be a China Coast bum, but I don't like to think I'm old yet.'

They were silent for some time. Dimitri eyed her sideways. Her hair was done up in a knot on top of her head, as it had been when he first met her. The upswept hair brought out the slender lines of her neck. She seemed quite unembarrassed by the silence that had come between them and by his observation of her, which she surely sensed.

He took a breath. 'Will you meet me for lunch tomorrow?'

She turned her head slowly to look at him. Her eyes seemed thoughtful, almost abstracted. 'Why should I?'

'I suppose I'm trying to pick you up, that's all.'

The uncertain smile came and went.

'Well?'

'I will think about it,' she said precisely.

'How did you come to be here anyway? Do you know Jan and Lisa?'

'No. Mr Sternor asked me.'

'Reuben Sternor? Why does a pretty girl like you come with an old goat like him?' He looked down. 'I'm sorry, that really was impertinent, wasn't it?'

But she did not resent his question, only lifting her eyebrows again as she said in her over-articulated English 'There are many reasons for that too.'

'What a mysterious person you are.'

'No, not mysterious.'

The verandah door swung open again with a sudden bang. One of the young police officers' heads craned round it. 'Curfew's on again. Afraid it's stay here all night, or go home now. The mob's out in force tonight.'

Inside the room, the chattering had been hushed, but now it rose again, excited and louder. Jan was standing by the phone, holding the receiver to one ear, covering the other with his hand. He was frowning and grimacing, his tired eyes screwed up tight in the loose folds of skin. Lisa stood silently beside him, hands clasped in front of her, watching his face.

MORE VIOLENCE ON ISLAND: TWO SHOT DEAD

Hong Kong Island experienced another night of serious rioting last night, despite the clamp-down of a curfew at eleven p.m. Police opened fire on a mob rampaging in Western District and killed two ring-leaders on the spot. Police spokesmen said last night that both men were found to have lethal daggers made from triangular files on their persons.

Picture (right) shows one of the dead men, with a bullet wound in centre of his chest. He was inciting rioters to resist the police when orders were given to open fire.

'You've changed your hair-style.'

'You do not approve?'

'You'd look good however you did it.'

'Oh. Thank you.'

'But it would be best of all if you just let it fall free.'

'Tell me about yourself.'

'What do you want to know?'

'Do you like spring rolls?'

'Thank you. What do you want to know?'

'Well, last night you said something about coming and going to Hong Kong. What did you mean? Are you a beautiful spy or something? Mata Hari?'

'Not so exciting.'

'Well?'

'My mother brought me to Hong Kong when the communists took over China. I was five. My father stayed behind.'

'Why?'

'He was a teacher. He thought he might be useful to them.'

'What did be teach?'

'Engineering.'

'And was he useful?'

'They would not let him join the party because his father had been a landlord. But they wanted him to teach. It was all right at first. But my mother did not want to stay. I went to school in Hong Kong.'

'Did you ever go back?'

'Oh yes. Every year. Then I went to London for four years. Ballet school.'

'Did you like it?'

'At first I was lonely. Then I liked it. Then my mother died and I went back to Shanghai. I danced there for a time, until I came back to Hong Kong.'

'What was it like? Did you have to dance political things?'

'Most of the time, yes. The acrobatics are good but the dancing if not too good.'

'Is that why you came back?'

'No. My father lost his job before the Cultural Revolution. He was in prison for a time. Then I could not dance any more ... Why he lost his job? He said that the American — what do you call them? Bobbins? — there were some left over from the old days and he said they were better than the Chinese ones. So they put him in prison for a time ... Yes, it is hard for him now ... How I got out? My father wanted me to go. He still had some friends in the party. They protected him. They helped me to get out ... I don't know, they have all been purged now. I hardly write any more, it can be dangerous for him. But sometimes I get news, from him or other people. No, he has not got his teaching job back.'

'I? No, I did not come to Hong Kong to dance. There is nothing here to speak of. I apply for a visa to go to England and dance there. I am in transit, like most of the people here ... Was I smiling? No, I did not know ... I applied six months ago now, but I have not heard anything yet.'

'Dimitri? That is a Russian name, isn't it?'

'My mother was Russian. Her father was a White Russian officer. He drifted down from Peking and opened a restaurant here ... She met my father and they got married, before the war. He was English, in the bank ... No, he died in Stanley, in the internment camp ... She's dead too, now. She used to run a sort of dress shop after the war. It never made much money ... No, I used to come and go, too. I was sent to boarding school in England. My English grandparents paid the fees ... And then I went to Cambridge, and then I came here ... Yes, and I got married and had two children...'

'No, two, the elder one's a boy ...'

'At Cambridge? Russian and Chinese.'

'Yes, I'm writing a stupid book about the Russian influence on Chinese literature. Why stupid? Because nearly everything I do is stupid ... As a matter of fact I suppose I am in transit too, yes. I've just applied for a job in London, anyway ...'

'Tell me more about yourself.'

'There is not any more.'

I can't get used to your hair like that.'

'Is it so bad? You call it pigtails, don't you?'

'Not bad at all, Different. Tell me about your day. How do you spend your time?'

'I get up in the morning.'

'What time?'

'About seven.'

'And then?'

'I go to the TV studios.'

'Don't you eat?'

'Yes, I have some breakfast. Why do you ask so many questions?'

'Many reasons. And then? Why are you smiling again?'

'Am I? Because you stole my line.'

'And then what?

'In the afternoon I teach your daughter.'

'And about a hundred other daughters.'

'Not all yours.'

'I hope not. And in the evening?'

'I go out or read. I always read before I go to bed.'

'What do you read?'

'All sorts of things. If I do not read, I do not feel harmonious.'

'Harmonious.'

'Is that the wrong word?'

'No ... No, it's a perfect word.'

They came out of the restaurant into the brilliant stare of the afternoon sun. For a few moments, Dimitri did not realize what was wrong, and then he stopped. The normally crowded street was nearly empty and many of the shops had their shutters up. Nothing but a few people standing on the street corners and one or two cars speeding past, going away from Central. This locked-in, waiting silence came only before a typhoon. Or a riot.

Mila was frowning. 'More trouble.'

'Let's go by the side-streets.'

At first it sounded like a football crowd, but then the waves of shouting and chanting became wilder and more ragged. A police siren or ambulance was screaming along the waterfront. Every street they turned down was blocked by a police cordon, so that they could guess the size of the crowd by the area that was cordoned off. The heart of the riot must have been in Edinburgh Place, where the cross-harbour ferry terminal was. It was there that the chanting and sporadic fierce bursts of shouting seemed loudest. And it was somewhere above there that the two helicopters were hovering, their clattering, scything blades glinting in the sun.

Dimitri thought they could skirt the riot by passing round the cricket ground and edging into the ferry terminal from the east. But as they were going past the Hilton Hotel, a mob suddenly boiled up the side-street by the Bank of China, hurling stones and bottles which splintered glass all over the road. Dimitri saw the gleam of knives. He hurried Mila into the hotel.

The Sikh doorman opened the grille to let them through and just had time to slam it shut and lock it again. The crowd surged past, shouting and chanting. Some of them tried to rush the grille, but it was too strong for them. A cloud of bottles and stones clattered and smashed against it and then they were gone.

A group of elderly American tourists stood watching from the shelter of the hotel lobby. One of them, a thickset man with rimless glasses and a camera dangling from his neck, moved closer to Dimitri.

'Say, what's going on?'

'I don't know, just a riot.'

'What're they rioting about? Are they communists?'

'I suppose some of them are. Most of them are just rioting.'

'What about?,

He shrugged. 'All sorts of things.'

'Huh. Well they're sure spoiling our trip here. We're booked on a junk tour and we can't even get out of the hotel.'

The noise of the crowd was coming nearer again. They were being slowly rolled back by two lines of riot police. The crowd stopped, taunted them, flung their bottles and stones, then scattered and ran as the police baton-charged, re-forming again twenty or thirty yards further back.

'Looks like a school bun fight,' the American chuckled.

'Does it?'

They were ebbing back past the iron grille now, shaking the bars and jeering at the onlookers. They were young, perhaps between sixteen and twenty-five. Some, more disciplined, wore Mao badges. These had their arms linked and chanted Mao-slogans. Others, the most part, seemed only out for violence. The showers of bottles and stones came mainly from them. A group of them began taunting Mila standing close to Dimitri, stabbing their fingers at her through the grille and calling her a white-skinned pig's whore. She stared back at them unblinkingly, only turning a bracelet ceaselessly round and round her wrist. Watching their faces, Dimitri understood the American's remark. They seemed to be smiling and laughing while they jeered, which made it look to Western eyes as though they were only joking. But the stiff alertness in Mila's stare showed that she knew better.

Suddenly they left the grille. The police were regrouping for another charge, but that was not the reason. A middle-aged Chinese had appeared between the police and the mob and started to harangue the rioters, waving his arms about madly. At first Dimitri thought he was a Maoist, but then he heard the words 'Communist gangsters' and realised the man must be some unbalanced nationalist.

'What's going on?' asked the American, taking out a cigar.

It was all finished in a few seconds. The mob closed round the man like dogs round a fox. The police came charging forward. The mob held for a moment and then swept back, leaving the man sprawled face down on the ground, very still and very small.

When the mob had gone, two policemen stayed behind, looking down at the man indifferently. He had not moved. Blood was slowly staining his shirt in several places and a dark pool of it widened steadily on the ground beneath him.

The American left, muttering something about his wife.

It was some time before the ambulance arrived. When the attendants put the man on the stretcher, they covered his face. Several press photographers had appeared by then. They went on snapping till the doors were closed and the ambulance started moving away. Then they snapped the blood on the road.

The ferries had stopped running. Dimitri and Mila took a walla-walla boat, which charged them five dollars instead of the normal one. The harbour was quiet and peaceful, as full of ships as ever, as if nothing could ever disturb it. The water slapped against the hull of the launch and rocked them gently. A light, cool breeze blew on their faces. Only the prowling helicopters, over Wanchai now, showed that the riot was still going on.

Dimitri watched Mila, letting his hand trail in the warm water. She sat looking at the approaching shore of Kowloon, still turning the bracelet on her wrist, but absently now. They had hardly spoken since the man was killed. Death, like love, seemed to make words superfluous. The wind plucked at her hair. Her pigtails lifted stiffly. Perhaps sensing his observation of her, she glanced across at him.

He moved closer. 'Not a very auspicious beginning, was it?'

'Beginning of what?'

He was gazing past her into the smooth, blue-green swell of the sea. 'Of whatever's going to happen next,' he said slowly.

She looked away again, neither grave nor smiling, narrowing her eyes against the sunlight. Then she reached up to untie her pigtails, shaking her hair loose as the ribbons came undone.

A boy of about ten, son of the helmsman, looked up from where he was squatting over his homework and watched her curiously. Her hair, falling halfway down her back, streamed and fluttered in the breeze.

PLA MOVEMENTS ON FRONTIER?
RENEWED DEMONSTRATIONS IN PEKING

Unconfirmed reports in leftist papers yesterday spoke of massive troop movements by elements of the People's Liberation Army on the border with Hong Kong. A British Forces spokesman contacted last night said he was unable to comment. Meanwhile, in Peking, the British Embassy was again the scene of day-long demonstrations by thousands of Red Guards, who marched past in column after column, shouting protests and chanting quotations from Chairman Mao. The walls of the mission were plastered with big character posters denouncing 'British Fascist Imperialism' for 'Vile Provocations and Atrocities' in Hong Kong.

'Why don't you take the children swimming if you've got nothing better to do? You're hardly ever here in the afternoons now, they practically never see you. It might just as well be your term time.'

'Are you coming?'

'What for? We'd only squabble. I've got too much to do here, anyway...'

'You just *make* work, Helen. Why the hell won't you let go? Just once?'

'If I did let go, I'd never start again.'

The children were playing listlessly in the mosquito-ridden shade at the back of the flats. Alexander was throwing stones into the dried-up nullah, whilst Elena made sour, sulky comments on his aim. Dimitri sent them up to change and got the car out of the garage. A mosquito flitted to and fro in front of his face. He clapped his hands, missed, clapped again and squashed it. A little drop of blood spurted out from the crushed delicate-striped body. He looked at both the body and the blood on his hand, then wiped them off on his handkerchief.

' 'mitri, why don't you get a new car?' Elena climbed past him into the back seat. 'This old Mini's much too squashy.'

' 's not. 's got a jolly good engine,' Alexander said importantly. 'Trouble is you can't tell a good engine when you see one.'

'Well it's still too squashy anyway.'

'Yeah, 'cos you're so fat.'

'Shut up both of you or I won't take you,' Dimitri said with perfunctory irritation. The threat, they all knew, was empty.

And they started off, the children scooping air in with their hands through the open windows. Dimitri glanced at them in the driving mirror as the car rolled down the steep hill towards Aberdeen. The wind blew their long fair hair across their foreheads. They were kneeling in their swimsuits on the back seat, gazing out of the windows at the steep green hills of the Dairy Farm pastures on one side and the sun-burnished sea on the other.

What do they know about Helen and me? he wondered, and saw no hint of an answer in their dreaming, open gaze. Well, we made some beautiful children if we did nothing else. He glanced away at the barren slopes of Lamma Island, a mile from the coast, and the fishing fleet from Aberdeen streaming out southwards towards the fishing grounds.

The road swung down into Aberdeen, past the grey terraced cemetery overlooking the sea. A road block, manned by police with rifles, was just round the corner. When they saw he was a foreign devil, they waved him past.

'Looking for rioters,' Alexander said, importantly again.

'Are there any rioters in Aberdeen, Dimitri?' Elena looked at him anxiously. Newspaper pictures of the dead and dying had worked on her imagination and she was afraid to go out by herself now, even in the safe area where they lived.

'No, I suppose they're just checking, though,' he answered casually, 'Just to make sure.' And there slipped into his mind the memory of that first death he had seen in his life, the Chinese policeman shot by the Japanese soldier. A memory which had not come to him until years later, in his English public school, as if it had been a time bomb buried in his brain, set to explode when he was loneliest and most unhappy. Then it had come to him night after night, so that he had prayed feverishly that he might fall asleep before the image came with its hallucinatory terror. Would Elena have to go through that too?

'How did they know we weren't rioters?'

'That's one crime the Europeans don't commit in Hong Kong.'

''cos the rioters are against the Brits, stupid.' Alexander looked at Dimitri for approval. 'They're all communists.'

Elena was still troubled. 'Are we against the communists or for them? We're Brits, aren't we?'

They drove through the dirty, narrow streets of Aberdeen, with its junks berthed against the edge of the road, and went on past Deepwater and Repulse Bay to the secluded beach at South Bay. The children jumped out of the car and ran down to the sand while Dimitri parked. He drove the car under the outspread branches of a flame of the forest. Its brilliant red flowers were just beginning to droop and fall and there was a thin carpet of them on the ground. By the time he had walked down the little stone steps on to the burning sand, the children were already in the sea, splashing towards the life-guard who lolled on his catamaran, dozing under a wide straw hat.

There were not many people on the beach. Some slim Chinese youths and girls lay listening to a transistor at one end and a few European women sat under sunshades in the middle, infants grubbing beside them in the sand. A group of American sailors, recognisable by their crew-cuts, were sipping soft drinks at the other end, each with a bar-girl in an arrestingly brief swimsuit. Dimitri dropped the towels on the sand and walked cautiously over the pebbles into the water.

It was smooth and calm. One-foot waves rolled lazily in, curled and hovered the whole length of the shore, then gently broke, hissing quietly up over the wet sand and washing slowly back again. He stood on the edge a moment, watching the cool water ebb and flow past his ankles, feeling the sand move beneath his feet, then he waded in and swam out to the children. The sea grew cooler the further out he swam. They raced to the raft in the middle of the bay and climbed on to it. A jelly-fish lay on the matting floor. Someone must have ladled it out of the sea with a paddle or flipper. It lay still, an opaque quivering grey-white jelly, dying in the sun. The children knew better than to touch it — they had both been stung before, carrying the red weals on their bodies for several weeks. They began jumping and diving off the raft.

'Keep a look-out for any more jelly-fish.' Dimitri left them and swam back to the shore. He swam on his back, kicking up a shimmering spray and gazing up at the endless light blue of the sky, across which a jet liner was dropping down, seemingly soundlessly, like a giant falling bird. Looking back over his head, the water just ringing his eyes, he could see the flames of the forest lining the shore and the dark green hills lifting up behind, enclosing the beach in a crescent of peace and stillness that made it hard to believe in the reality of the riot he had seen from the Hilton a few weeks ago. Impossible to believe that that man had really been butchered before his eyes — *multiple stab wounds and lacerations*, the papers had said — only five miles from here.

He climbed out of the water, feeling his weight suddenly dragging him down again. The beach looked now as it must have looked a hundred years ago to the first European. Or two thousand years ago to the first fishermen, who had lived here then much as they lived now. Through all the centuries of Europe's conquest by the Romans, the barbarians, of the dark ages, the Renaissance and the industrial revolution, the sea had beaten upon this shore and the fishermen had gone out in junks and brought back their catch. I don't believe in progress, he thought as he spread out his towel. The onward march to what?

The children were still leaping off the raft into the sea, sending up cascades of spray. He lay back and closed his eyes. The sun dried the salt water off his skin and then enveloped him in drowsy heat. The slow, regular thump and swish of the waves on the sand, the cries of children and the tinny blare of radio music all grew fainter and more distant. He dozed.

The firm gentleness of Mila's body, the warm moistness of her lips, her mischievous tongue. The hollows he had explored, beneath her ear, beneath the delicate edge of her collar bone, between her breasts, around her navel, the shallow sweeping curve of her hips, the dimples in her buttocks and the arching hollows of her insteps with their fine blue veins spreading under the pale skin. The long slow curve of her back and the shadowy hollows beneath her shoulder blades, under her arms — 'No, I am ticklish'- and the small brown nipples hardening against his tongue. To make a woman move with joy so easily, so simply — how was it possible? To feel so loose ... I had forgotten that could be ...

The twang of American voices and the crunch of sand awoke him. The sailors were leaving, each with his girl. Suddenly he saw Julie, in white shorts and a red blouse. She saw him too, and half-waved, irresolute. He beckoned her across and she left her sailor, a small young-looking blond man with an uncertain ginger moustache.

'Hi.' She touched his shoulder with her bare foot. Her toenails were varnished bright red to match her blouse.

'Who's your friend?' he asked in Cantonese. He shook her foot as if it had been her hand. 'How do you do?'

She laughed. Her laugh always reminded him of Blacks' voices, Not the high, bell-like laugh of Chinese girls. 'Huh. He's a sailor. Aircraft carrier. Leaves for Vietnam tomorrow.'

'Does he have a lot of money?'

She laughed again. 'Not any more.'

'Don't get caught in a riot with him, Julie.'

She wrinkled her nose disdainfully. 'I don't make trouble for them, so why should they make trouble for me?'

'Be careful anyway. I saw a man killed not long ago.'

But she only shrugged, disdainfully again. She looked around. 'Wife not here?'

'Home.'

'Always home, eh?' She looked at him shrewdly.

'Those are my kids out there.'

'Yes, I saw them.' She gazed out at the raft and smiled.

There was a hesitant reticence between them for a few seconds. Mila had unwittingly withdrawn him from Julie. He looked down at her toes curling and uncurling in the sand.

The other girls were calling her. She turned to go.

'You come and see me soon, eh?' She slipped into her pidgin English. 'Long time no see.'

'Sure.' He felt uneasy at the almost pleading tone in her voice. She liked people she could rely on, who would see her regularly.

He watched her saunter back to the others, then lowered his head on the towel again.

An image of her rose behind his eyes as he closed them. He saw her on the bed in her room in Timshatsui, taking a cheque from him wonderingly. 'I can't take this to the bank.'

'Why not?'

'They will laugh at me!'

But he had persuaded her to take it and watched her shyly cash it in the Central Branch. She had gazed up at the ornate vaulted ceiling with as much awe as if it had been a cathedral. And she had come away from the counter with the money in her hand, smiling like a child after her first communion. It was then that the thought had come to him that the Hong Kong and Shanghai Bank should have been dubbed The First Church of Mammon in Hong Kong.

That was more than a year ago, when he had first known her. She must have her own account by now.

The children came running out of the sea, their feet slapping on the wet sand. The water glistened on their bodies and their hair hung down in long wet tangles. Oh God, don't do anything to hurt them, he told himself — or was it prayed? — with an obscure throbbing anxiousness, as he watched them racing towards him.

'Dimitri, who was that lady?' Alexander shook himself like a dog.

'Oh, just a friend ... She used to be a student of mine.'

'Was that man her boy-friend?'

'I expect so.'

Elena giggled. 'No, Dimitri's her boy-friend, I bet he is.'

'You don't have girl-friends when you've married, stupid. Don't you know that yet?'

Dimitri busied himself with the towels. 'Come on, we'll be late for dinner.'

Some more flowers had fallen from the flame of the forest. Elena collected them off the bonnet and roof of the car while Alexander spread the towels over the seats.

'Come on, the mosquitoes are biting.'

The evening sun shone into Dimitri's eyes now as he drove, dazzling although no longer fierce. The police at the road block waved him through again. They were checking the passengers in a lorry from one of the communist stores. Elena held her nose as they passed the Aberdeen Fish Market with its Union Jack drooping over the ugly concrete sheds which the government had put up.

On the long hill up from Aberdeen, Dimitri looked again at the green hilly meadows and low whitewashed cattle sheds of Dairy Farm, tinted a warm mellow pink now by the setting sun. A line of black-clothed peasant women with wide Hakka hats was loping down one of the steep hillside paths towards the road. They carried long bamboo poles on their shoulders with big bales of fresh-cut grass balanced at each end. The chattering of their shrill, high voices, almost like the cries of birds, sounded above the straining grind of the engine. For a moment he saw them outlined black against the fading sky, jogging one after the other, their long poles bending and swaying, giving a little upward spring to their step, as if they were dancing some elaborate harvest dance like the Balinese danced with their rice bowls. The sun's low-slanting rays gleamed on their sweating brown and wrinkled faces and they looked like stained, carved wood. Then they were gone as the car laboured over the top of the hill.

The children were drowsy now. They climbed out slowly and walked heavily to the lift, dragging their towels behind them. Elena carried her red flowers half-crushed in one hand. Dimitri locked the car door and followed them, gazing at their sea-tangled hair and fair, sunburned skins. Oh God, don't do anything to hurt them, he thought again.

Suddenly, as if by arrangement, the cicadas began chirping in the grass and in the trees all round — the long, jarring, yet peaceful music of tropical nights.

PEKING CLAIMS HONG KONG

Peking radio yesterday broadcast 'an important message to all compatriots in Taiwan, Hong Kong and Macau' in which Chinese sovereignty over all these territories was formally and unambiguously declared. The message, which was broadcast at dictation speed — used only rarely, and exclusively for extremely important announcements — after declaring that Taiwan, Hong Kong and Macau were 'inalienable parts of the People's Republic of China' went on to advise patriotic compatriots' to await the day which was soon to come when they would be 'returned to the great motherland'.

Observers were uncertain whether this was in effect a threat of immediate take-over, or merely a repetition of the position which Peking has always held about Hong Kong and Macau on the one hand, and Taiwan on the other. However, it was generally agreed that the broadcasting of such a message, particularly at dictation speed, was 'unusual'. One source even described it as 'ominous'.

Dimitri walked past the big communist store in Nathan Road. It was midday, but the windows were shuttered and the doors barred. Large-character posters denouncing the *'Hong Kong British Bandits'* and blown-up photographs of injured rioters were stuck on every free space. A large red banner quoting Chairman Mao was strung the length of the building, across all the first-floor windows.

The forces of socialism have become overwhelmingly superior to the forces of imperialism.

Looking up higher, he saw several faces peering down at him through barred windows. A police Landrover drove slowly past, its windows and lamps covered with wire mesh. Four policemen sat helmeted in the back. They were scanning the building, rifles across their knees. The faces behind the upstairs windows stared sullenly back.

The street was almost empty and tensely still, as if another riot was forming. Dimitri realised that there was no other European in view. He walked on quickly and turned down the next side street. The feeling of exposed isolation and danger that he had felt outside the Hilton came over him now with stronger force. He sensed a hundred unseen eyes focused on his back as he walked quickly along the sun-scorched pavement.

Mila lived in a seedy, paint-peeling block near Nathan Road. The lift shook and creaked complainingly, smelling of heat and vague, unspecifiable dirt. Looking upwards past the ineffective fan in the roof, Dimitri watched the frayed and ungreased cable quivering as it slowly wound him up, then juddered to a halt.

He stepped out into the musty corridor. A stunted rubber plant stood forlorn outside her door, its leaves coated with a glutinous layer of dust. The dry earth in its pot was littered with squashed and crumpled cigarette ends.

Mila opened the door before he could press the bell, a hairbrush in her hand. Her hair had just been loosened from the Grecian knot she wore when dancing. She was still wearing her leotard and tights. She looked at him in her grave, considering way, then smiled. 'I saw you crossing the road.'

'What a squalid building you live in.' He took the brush from her hand.

Her heavy lids drooped slowly in exaggerated disdain. 'It is only because you have never seen a real slum.'

'You think so?' He began stroking her hair with the brush, arranging a parting in the middle of her head. 'As a matter of fact, I've probably seen more slums than you have.'

'Ah. But you have not lived in them.' She looked up again, smiling. 'I saw you crossing the road.'

'That means you must have been watching for me.' He let the brush glide down to the end of her hair and then started stroking her breast and belly. 'Aren't you going to ask me in?'

'Actually, I was expecting there would be a riot.'

'So was I. The communist store was all barred and bolted like a fort. It made me feel creepy, the streets were so empty.'

She stayed his hand as he brushed downwards. 'If there is trouble, you must not come here.'

'I can't stop myself at the moment. You must tell your commie friends to stop rioting.'

'You must tell your fascist friends to stop persecuting my patriotic compatriots.'

'Aren't you going to ask me in?'

She placed her hands against his chest. 'Perhaps this place is too squalid for you?'

He glanced past her at the bright orange cushions scattered over the teak floor, with the large white goatskin in the middle. The little ceiling fan whirred quietly above it. 'I think I might be able to put up with it for a couple of hours.' He pulled her close, throwing the hair-brush into the room.

'Arrogant neo-colonial fascist bandit,' she murmured as his lips felt for hers.

'Provocative leftist disturber of law and order.'

Her body moulded itself to his as though she had melted against him. He kissed her lips and her throat and her closed, slanting eyes. Her eyelids trembled under his tongue. He pushed her gently inside and shut the door with his foot. Her breath rose unevenly in his ear and then her lips were on his again.

They collapsed on the goatskin. And again she was so loose and free, her desire so spontaneous and giving, that he felt a kind of awed wonder at the existence of such freshness, such uncomplicated joy.

Afterwards he lay looking up at the ceiling, sweating and peacefully exhausted. Mila's head rested on his shoulder. She was breathing quietly. He watched the fan blades slowly spinning round and round, wafting a little cool air over their bodies. A police siren wailed somewhere far away, but the street outside was still unnaturally quiet. The fan blades slowly turned, his gaze fixed on the metal boss, which seemed almost motionless, and his watching eyes grew hazed and blurred.

Her head moved. She nuzzled his throat.

'I thought you were asleep?'

'I was. Were you?'

'Just thinking.'

'Thinking what?' She stroked the hair on his chest and belly, still moist with sweat. 'Thinking what, my furry beast?'

He glanced down at her head. Her hair veiled her eyes. He brushed it aside.

'Thinking what?'

'Tell me about Reuben Sternor.'

'Ah.' Her eyelids lowered. 'You are jealous.'

'No ... just interested.'

She curled the dark hair on his chest round her forefinger while she spoke. 'He has a relative in London who is connected with the ballet companies ... Perhaps he can help me to get a job.'

'Oh.'

'Because without a job, I cannot get a work permit.'

'And without a work permit you can't get a visa. And without a visa you can't get to London?'

She nodded. 'I have a British passport but since it is issued in Hong Kong I am only a second-class British subject.'

'Yes, I know the deal.'

She tugged at the hair she had wound round her fingers. 'Are you angry?'

'Why should I be?' He shook his head. 'Do you have a Chinese passport too?'

'Yes. Of course.'

He was watching the boss of the fan as it smoothly turned. 'Do you and Reuben... ?'

She shook her head. 'He does not want that.'

'Yet?'

She lifted herself suddenly on her elbow, looking down at him, the seriousness of her eyes relieved by a mocking smile round her lips. 'Now you are jealous. You think I am a whore.'

He laughed, pulling her down on top of him. 'If you were, you wouldn't be the first I've known. And liked.'

'*Aiya*.' She sighed comically, in Cantonese.

'Besides, are you jealous of Helen?'

'Your wife?' She continued in Cantonese. 'No. Why should I be? It's not the custom for concubines to be jealous of wives.'

'That's what you think.' He too slipped into Cantonese. 'Considering you come from Shanghai, your Cantonese isn't bad.'

'Considering you were born here, yours is terrible.'

He bit her throat for answer, nipping the skin between his teeth.

'How did you meet your wife?'

'Helen? I met her through Peter Frankam, actually. She was playing in a concert at Cambridge and he introduced me afterwards. He was keen on her. I think he thought she was a cultural asset.'

'And why did you marry her?'

'Is it so obvious that my marrying her needs an explanation?' He let his fingers run slowly down Mila's back. 'Why does anyone marry anyone? At the time it seemed the thing to do.' He laughed, wrily. 'We thought that she would be a great pianist and I would be a great scholar. Look at us now.'

'Are you not a great scholar?' She had her elbows on his chest and held her chin in her hands looking down, at him quizzically. Her hair hung straight down each side of her face, reaching his shoulders. 'Aren't you?'

'No. I don't try hard enough, for one thing.'

'Why not? I would try hard for dancing.'

'Now, yes. But five years from now?'

She only lifted her brows disbelievingly and shrugged. Then she looked down at him again. 'What about your book?'

'My stupid book? It's just trying to see what influence the Russians have had on Chinese literature ... I think their style always remained alien really. That's what I try to explain, why it never really caught on. Let's talk about something else.'

'Why?'

'Because books about books are usually boring. Mine is, anyway. I just drifted into this business because I started off knowing Russian and Chinese, you see. I'm just lazy really, that's all.'

'What would you rather do?'

'I'm doing it now.' He smiled at her smile. I have a simple idea of the good life, very simple ... It's a sort of drowsy contemplativeness ... Like just now ... I was absolutely still, just watching the fan going round, and round, and round ... Absorbed in it ... Nothing else. If only that state were eternal ... And love, too ... Yes, love. As it is with you ... Because that has a kind of stillness too...'

She smiled, half-mocking, half-serious. 'You sound like a Buddhist in search of Nirvana. Or an opium-smoker.'

'And music too ... that also has its tranquillity, sometimes. Not books though, not literature. Words are too restless, too spiky ... They have meanings. Except some poetry, that's all right...'

The mockery in her smile displaced the seriousness as she gazed down at him. 'And what about painting? And dancing? A scholar like you, even if you are not a very good scholar, you ought not to leave anything out.'

'Bitch.' He took her hair and wound it round her throat. 'I ought to throttle you for that.'

But she let her head fall till her moist lips were on his. Their finger-tips went stroking indolently over each other's skin while their lips and tongues played. Then, from languidness their desire flared suddenly into ferocity. Dimitri plunged into her again and again, while she clawed and bit him, laughed, moaned, shuddered and sighed.

FIVE HONG KONG POLICEMEN KILLED IN BORDER CLASH WITH CHINA TROOPS RUSHED TO SHA TAU KOK

Five policemen were shot dead at Sha Tau Kok yesterday and several seriously wounded, when the police post and rural committee building were fired upon by machine-guns from the Chinese side of the border. Gurkha troops and a squadron of armoured cars were brought up late in the afternoon to rescue the remaining seventy policemen, who had been pinned down by murderous automatic cross-fire for most of the afternoon.

The incident began when several hundred demonstrators stormed across the border and began throwing stones and fish-bombs at the police post. Some wooden projectiles and tear-gas shells were fired to disperse the mob, whereupon the police were cut down by a hail of bullets from across the border. A senior police official said this morning that the Hong Kong Police at no time fired back across the border. 'It is ridiculous,' he said. 'They have only revolvers and riot guns. What could they do against heavy machine guns? In any case, the frontier police are under strict orders never to fire across the border. That is a military matter, not for police to handle.'

It is understood that Government is seriously concerned that similar incidents and shootings could occur anywhere along the thirty mile frontier, any one of which might involve the armed forces of both sides. It is felt that the Colony faces its gravest threat since the Japanese invasion.

Leave for police and troops was cancelled yesterday. Auxiliary police and members of the Hong Kong Regiment have been ordered to report for duty.

PROVOCATIONS BY BRITISH AUTHORITIES IN HONG KONG

On July 8, people on our side of Sha Tau Kok and Chinese inhabitants of the 'New Territories' in Kowloon held a rally on our side to voice support for our patriotic countrymen in Hong Kong and Kowloon in their just struggle, against brutal persecution by the British authorities in Hong Kong. When the Chinese inhabitants were returning to the 'New Territories', fully-armed policemen and 'riot-police' of the British Authorities in Hong Kong carried out a premeditated sanguinary suppression of them, throwing tear-gas bombs and opening fire on them, and at the same time fired at our side.

The Chinese frontier guards at once fired warning shots against such atrocities and provocations. But, in total disregard of the warnings from our side, the policemen and 'riot-police' of the British authorities in Hong Kong continued to fire at the demonstrators, killing one and wounding eight of them.

Our frontier guards also fired back at the policemen and 'riot-police' of the British Authorities in Hong Kong.

'What will you do if the mainland takes over Hong Kong?'

'It is not a question what *I* will do,' Mila was gazing out of the car window at the darkened, narrow streets by the harbour. 'It is what *they* will do that is the question.' She turned the quarter light to slide more air into the car. 'You should not drive this way, it is dangerous.'

'It's quicker. Besides, everywhere is equally dangerous, now that they've started throwing bombs.'

'Elena did not come to her lesson this afternoon.'

'No, Helen's keeping her at home. Did many children stay away?'

'Especially the Chinese girls. Their parents are more worried than the Europeans are.'

'They've more reason to be. They'll be first on the list if the communists do take over. Especially if the Red Guards are in control. Why do you -?'

'Look.' Mila nodded ahead. 'I told you it was dangerous.'

Far down the street, the red lights of police vans turned and winked like angry eyes. Police were strung out along the pavement and across the road. As Dimitri drove slowly nearer he saw a dark mass of demonstrators being pressed back by a triple line of riot police.

He stopped by a police van when its driver waved him down.

The driver shone his torch over them and glanced at Mila estimatingly.

'Tell your boy-friend we're just picking up some communist pigs,' he said in Cantonese. 'No need to worry.'

Dimitri smiled. Whenever a Chinese girl was seen with a European man, it was usually assumed she was a bar-girl. The belief that a girl would have to be depraved to want to go with a European went both wide and deep, especially among Chinese men.

Mila gave the policeman a cool, expressionless glance, then turned her head away. 'My husband speaks Cantonese perfectly,' she said quietly.

The policeman, discomfited, moved back.

'If only that had been true,' Dimitri said slowly.

'What?' She smiled teasingly. 'About Cantonese?'

'About husband. You knew that.'

She looked back at the lines of police without answering.

The police outnumbered the demonstrators this time. The demonstrators were pinned back against a wall and snatch squads of police hauled them away one by one into the waiting vans. A burly European inspector and a Chinese corporal dragged a youth into the van beside them. The youth could not have been more than twenty. The inspector drew his revolver as they pulled him up the two steps and the corporal kicked him in the back. The soft smacking thud of metal on flesh and wordless, muffled screams came out of the van before the door slammed shut. Dimitri heard the inspector's voice saying calmly, in Cantonese, 'Put the boot in again,' and then some more dull thuds, like someone kicking a mattress. But there were no more screams.

Two more police arrived, dragging a man with a gash over his eye. The inspector and the corporal came out. The inspector was holding his gun by the barrel. Two other policemen slammed the door of the van shut behind them.

'They are having their revenge,' Mila said, an icy stillness in her voice.

'Have you got a pencil?'

'Why?'

'Their numbers. The numbers on their shoulders. Quick.'

A sharp high scream sounded abruptly through the open, barred windows of the van door.

RIOTS — NO LET-UP

More than thirty people were arrested last night when an unruly crowd disobeyed a police order to disperse. Several received injuries whilst resisting arrest. Knives, clubs and two home-made bombs were found on the ground when order was restored at half past eleven. The bombs were detonated on the spot as they were considered too dangerous to be moved. Traffic was held up for over an hour.

Sha Tau Kok had another quiet day. Gurkha troops are patrolling the area in company with the police. At another border post, however, Man Kam To, about two hundred people from the Chinese side of the frontier bombarded the police post with rocks, bamboo stakes and fish bombs. One policeman received injuries and was taken to hospital in Fan Ling.

CULTURAL REVOLUTION IN MORE TROUBLE?

Unconfirmed reports were received yesterday of heavy fighting between rival military factions in China's industrial city of Wuhan. Artillery and paratroops are said to have been brought into action. It is understood that the military governor of Wuhan had refused to implement directives from the Red Guards and had instead put many of them in prison.

A family of five who escaped from the mainland in a stolen junk yesterday told marine police that nobody knew any more who was in power in China. Despite the disturbances in Hong Kong, refugees continue to flood in at the rate of two or three hundred a month.

In Hong Kong, there was serious rioting on both sides of the harbour, and two men who disobeyed orders to stop when seen carrying suspicious parcels were shot. One of the men arrested in the previous day's disturbances has died in custody. An inquest is to be held.

Lok Ma Chau, by the Chinese border. A little round hill lifting up from the flat, marshy plain which the Shum Chun river flows through. Mila and Dimitri lean on the white wooden fence under the shade of a willow tree. Further up the hill, on the very top, stands the whitewashed and sandbagged police post, Union Jack slapping against its mast. Coils of newly laid barbed wire surround it. Below them, the hill slopes steeply down to the looping river which is the frontier. Gurkha soldiers are repairing the ten-foot wire fence. Heaps of red earth scar the green, where machine-gun nests have been dug and sandbagged. Their guns cover the single unmade road that leads past the British checkpoint, red and white barrier, through no-man's-land to the Chinese check-point, white barrier. In the no-man's-land is a large duck farm. The ducks' quacking, cracked and mournful, sounds clearly up the hill, is stilled, then rises again.

A sentry by the Chinese check-point watches the Gurkhas through binoculars. In the fields behind, large red flags flutter where the peasants are working. A truck drives slowly along the road inside China, churning up a cloud of reddish-yellow dust. The whining noise of its engine drifts up the hill too, carried by the wind. The truck is driving towards the town of Shum Chun, for the road leads nowhere else. It recedes slowly and the cloud of dust almost hides it. Then it disappears altogether as the road curls out of sight behind a tree-covered hill. They watch the dust settling like a flock of birds over the fields.

'It seems impossible that they were shooting near here a few weeks ago,' Dimitri says, tritely.

The old Hakka women who sell curios to tourists, and let themselves be photographed in their wide black-crowned hats for a dollar a time, have tried half-heartedly to interest Dimitri and Mila in their trinkets. Now they squat in the ugly little pavilion behind them and watch indifferently, occasionally spitting noisily on the ground.

'Have you ever been here before, Mila?'

She shakes her head. 'I usually pass through the border at Lowu.'

'I mean to the New Territories.'

She shrugs. 'I do not come. It is not my home.'

'A true Chinese.' He smiles. 'Some of my students have lived in Hong Kong all their lives and never even been to one of the outlying islands. Let alone Macau.'

'Nor have I.'

'I'll take you.'

'We are not as restless as you foreign devils.'

'Yet you have lived in London.'

'To study, yes. That is different. We are not tourists.'

A sudden flurry of quacking comes from the unseen ducks. Some dogs start barking wildly.

'What are you going to do about it?' Mila looks at him for the first time.

'How did you know that was on my mind?'

A faint shrug. 'What are you going to do about it?'

'There's only one thing *to* do, isn't there?' They are speaking in English, but their voices are lowered as if they are afraid the Hakka women might overhear and understand.

She is gazing at the heat-hazed mountains distantly bounding the Chinese plain. 'You will report it to someone?'

'To the police.'

She frowns slightly. Otherwise her face is still. 'But it was the police who did it.'

'So?'

But she does not follow her protest through. Instead, she comes closer to what is behind her doubtfulness. 'What will you tell them?'

'What we saw. What we saw and heard.' His voice is touched with impatience. He has felt all the time she will pull back. That is why at first he has delayed speaking about it, why now he is bristling already at her indirect reluctance.

'Do not say what *we* saw and heard. Say what *you* saw and heard.'

'Why?'

She ignores the sharpness in his tone. 'Because I cannot afford to be involved.'

'Oh? What do you mean by that?'

'I mean that it will make a lot of trouble for me and it will not do any good. So it is ... stupid.' Her voice too is hardening.

He looks at her, but she gazes unblinkingly away at the mountains, refusing to meet his eyes. One of the Hakka women behind them hawks loudly several times, then spits.

'Won't it do some good if someone is tried and found guilty, and everyone knows it?'

'It would, perhaps. But it will not happen.'

'Why not?' He cannot keep the coldness out of his voice.

'Because we are in Hong Kong ... And the communists and the riots ... There would only be much trouble and nothing happens.'

'In the first place,' he says cuttingly, 'you don't know that nothing will happen. And in the second place, the only trouble will be making a statement to the police. Is that bothering you too much?'

She is silent for some time, but seeing the pulse throb in her throat, he knows she is not calm. 'How will you explain to Helen how I came to be in your car?'

'As a matter of fact I've told her already.' He smiles with a certain malicious triumph. 'I told her I saw you at a bus-stop on the way home from the library and gave you a lift.'

'Ah.' She smiles too. 'You have protected yourself very well ... The trouble is, I cannot protect myself. If I went to the police with you, I would never get a visa for England.'

'Hong Kong's not as corrupt as that, Mila.' He laughs. 'That's ridiculous.'

'For you it is not as corrupt, because you are British.'

'I simply don't believe that anyone could prevent you from getting a visa if you got a work permit from London.'

'You have lived in Hong Kong a long time,' she speaks with a quiet scornfulness, 'and of course you have visited the New Territories and the islands. But still perhaps you do not know Hong Kong very well. Why should I sacrifice myself for someone I do not know, especially when it will do no good?'

Dimitri's eyes are set on two Gurkha soldiers oiling their machine-gun fifty yards beneath them. "The thing I can't stand about you Chinese, you traditional Chinese, is your total callousness about everyone except your own family or your own clan. If that's what they're trying to get rid of over there' — nodding across the river — 'Well, good luck to them, that's all.'

'It is not callous. And what do you know about "over there"? Do you think you can understand us because you have learnt a bit of our language?'

'I've heard all that cultural chauvinism before. *Ad nauseam.*'

Her face has become rigid. 'I will never get a visa if I am mixed up in this.'

'How do you know?'

'Because I am Chinese. And I have lived here a long time too. I will never get a visa. And how will it help the man, anyway? Do his family want you to meddle? You do not trouble to ask.' She falls into Cantonese, despite the Hakka women watching and listening. And instead of frigid exactness, she speaks now with a rush of fierce heat. 'You and your foreign justice! It's easy for you because all you're going to get out of it either way is a nice smug conscience. You're safe anyway because you're British. But for me it's different. Don't you know how your great British colony works yet? If you really care so much about it, why don't you give his family some money — something that's worth something?'

Dimitri has never seen her angry before. Her face is flushed under her fine, pale skin and her lips are set tight. He looks away at the border fence again. The Gurkhas beneath them are laughing quietly, the ducks quacking in the farm and the red flags of China fluttering still in the vast fields.

'Once, when I was in the internment camp, at Stanley ... in the war ...' he begins almost musingly, 'I saw them beat a man ... He'd been caught trying to escape . -. . The guards had these long bamboo clubs ... I can still hear the sound of them swishing and thudding ... They took it in turns. And one of them kept hissing through his teeth when he hit him. A sort of whistle of enjoyment ...'

He feels her looking at him while his own eyes dwell inwardly upon the pulped body that had lain like a sack in the afternoon sun.

'What happened to the man, Dimitri?'

He shrugs. 'He died too.'

She is still for a long time, only her eyes moving as she looks from the Gurkhas to the red flags and back at the unmade road to Shum Chun. At last she too shrugs, speaking in English again. 'I am sorry. I can't.'

GRUESOME FINDS IN FISHERMEN'S NETS

Fishermen hauled several corpses aboard their boats last night when fishing near the Pearl River estuary. The corpses were badly decomposed and had apparently been in the water for some time. Some had their hands tied behind their backs. All were dressed in the blue dungaree-type trousers worn in mainland China and there was speculation that they may have drifted down the Pearl River into the open sea.

A hydrofoil of the Hong Kong — Macau run also reported sighting a corpse yesterday in the same area. The vessel stopped and attempted to pick up the body, but it was too putrified to be handled. 'It dissolved when we touched it with the boat hook,' the coxswain Mr Albert Lo, told reporters. 'Nobody would handle it, so we left it to sink.'

Picture shows a shrouded body brought ashore aboard one of Hong Kong's trawlers. A trawler-owner said this morning that some crews were so shocked by the corpses that they had dumped the whole catch back into the sea.

In Hong Kong, three police constables were injured in separate bomb-throwing incidents yesterday. Two are in hospital. Their condition was described as 'serious'. The third was discharged after treatment.

The detective inspector in mufti looked more like a commercial traveller than a policeman. He thought long and carefully about the wording of the statement, gazing vacantly across the room with protuberant blue eyes while he absently fingered his ginger moustache before writing down each sentence.

When he had finished, he read it through to himself, following the lines with his heavy black pen. Dimitri noticed that his fingernails were badly bitten.

'There we are, Mr Johnston.' He looked up at Dimitri at last, glancing also at Mila, who sat in motionless hostility a little further away from his desk.

Dimitri leant forward to take the statement, but the inspector's hand was still on it.

'Of course, they've been under a lot of pressure...'

'Yes?'

'Five shot in Sha Tau Kok, bombs, stabbings ... That p.c. who had his throat ripped out with a cargo hook. Did you read about that Mr Johnston?'

'Yes I did.'

He was fingering his moustache again. 'I suppose they might be a little ... rough under those circumstances...'

'It was more than rough.'

'Yes, I know you *think* that.' His eyes were gazing ruminatively at Mila now. 'But you don't think anything happened, Miss Chan?'

'I said I did not see anything happen.'

'Or hear?'

'Or hear.'

'How was that?' He frowned down at Dimitri's statement as if there might be a clue there. 'How was that?'

'I have no idea. I was not looking at the police van.'

'But that wouldn't stop you hearing anything, would it? If there were loud cries?'

'There were a lot of noises. I did not notice anything in particular.'

'Would you like a cigarette?' He took a pack out of his shirt pocket and offered it to each of them. 'No? Well, let's see about *your* statement Miss Chan. You say you did see some people being arrested? Were they young or old?'

I, Dimitri Johnston, aged thirty-five, residing in West Rose Towers, Pokfulam Road in the colony of Hong Kong, do hereby state and declare:

At about ten-thirty on the night of July 29th, 1967, I was driving along Des Voeux Road West coming from the university in the direction of the vehicular ferry. Miss Mila Chan was a passenger in my car. At or near Rumsey Street I encountered some police action against a crowd of demonstrators. A police constable who appeared to be the driver of a large police van waved me to stop. I observed a European inspector and a Chinese corporal arresting a young man. I observed the inspector draw his revolver and the corporal kick the young man as he climbed the steps into the van. I heard sounds, which appeared to be that of striking and hitting come from the van. I heard a voice say in Cantonese 'Put the boot in again.' I heard some cries of pain. When the inspector and the corporal left the van I made a note of the corporal's number. The inspector did not have a number. I observed two Chinese constables push another man into the van and I heard similar sounds of what I took to be beating and shouts as of pain. Subsequently I recognised the photo of the first man to be taken into the van when it was published in the newspaper. When I discovered that the young man had died in custody, I went to the police.

Question How long did you see the face of the first man to be taken into the van?

Answer About five or six seconds.

Question How much light was there?

Answer The street lamps were shining.

Question Why did you think the sounds from the van were sounds of beating?

Answer I have heard beatings before, in Stanley Internment Camp.

Question Who do you think uttered the words 'Put the boot in again'?

Answer It sounded like a European speaking Cantonese, and I thought it was the European inspector.

Question Was it too dark for you to recognise the inspector again?

Answer I believe I would recognise him again.

I, Mila Chan, alias Chan Ling Kwan, aged twenty-three, residing in Lyttleton House, Kowloon, in. the colony of Hong Kong, do hereby state and declare:

At about ten-thirty on the night of July 29th, 1967, 1 was a passenger in a vehicle driven by Mr Dimitri Johnston. The car was stopped by a police constable at or near Rumsey Street whilst proceeding in the direction of the vehicular ferry. There were a large number of police dealing with a crowd of demonstrators. I heard a lot of noise but I did not notice any person being kicked and I did not hear any cries or shouts of pain.

Question Did you see any people being arrested?

Answer Yes.

Question Were any arrested persons placed in a police van near where the car you were travelling in was stopped?

Answer I believe so.

Question Did you see or hear anything which might lead you to suppose that unlawful violence was being used on any person in the police van next to you?

Answer I did not notice anything.

Question Were you looking at the police van?

Answer Most of the time I was not.

Question Did Mr Johnston say anything to you about what he thought was happening in the police van?

Answer He said that someone was being beaten up. But I did not notice anything.

TWO CHILDREN SLAIN IN BOMB OUTRAGE

In one of the most dastardly communist-inspired acts to date, two children, aged seven and two, were blown to pieces yesterday afternoon by a parcel bomb which they had picked up and started to play with.

The bomb had been left in Ching Wah Street, a cul de sac used as a children's playground. A seven year old girl, Wang Yee Man, apparently picked it up and carried it up the hill to a parked car. There, with her young two-year-old brother, Siu-Fan, she started to unwrap the parcel. There was a loud explosion and the car was wrecked. First on the scene was the children's father. He found his daughter terribly mutilated, with a hole in her stomach. She was dead. Shocked and dazed, he picked up his son, whose face was black with explosive, and ran down the hill. When an ambulance arrived, it was discovered that Siu-Fan was dead too.

Picture shows the grief-stricken father being comforted by relatives outside his shop last night.

It was noticed that leftist papers did not report the incident in their morning editions today.

A police spokesman again warned parents not to let their children play with any suspicious objects. 'Many of these devices are very powerful,' he said, 'and as they look like parcels they will be very tempting to children.' He described the planting of the bomb as 'cold-blooded and callous'.

' 'mitri, why don't you take us swimming any more?'

'I do, Alex. Only not so often. I've been working on this article.'

'Well is it finished then? What do you have to do it for, anyway?'

'Perhaps it is finished, just about…'

'Because Helen never takes us either. 's no fun. She's so scared of these stupid bombs. As if you'd be so crazy as to pick one up.'

'All right I'll take you on Sunday. Maybe we'll have a picnic at Twelve Mile Beach. How about that?'

They got out of the car as soon as they had parked on the ferry. The children ran forward to watch the waves slapping up and spraying over the boat's low, blunt bows. Helen and Dimitri stayed in the shade, leaning over the rail. A round grey-white jelly-fish drifted past the side of the boat, wallowing in the wash. It was dense and opaque, at least a foot across, somehow inertly malevolent and obscene.

'You're very preoccupied these days.' Helen's voice sounded half-questioning, half-accusing.

'Am I?'

'You have been for weeks. Is it about this police case?'

'No.' He was still watching the jelly-fish as it slipped slowly away. 'Out of my hands now, anyway.'

She leant back to look at the children. 'Are you worried about the bombs?'

'Not much. Are you?'

'One of the children could pick one up so easily.'

'Yes, but … He shrugged, glancing up at the white and dark ships lying so still in their berths throughout the harbour. 'I mean they don't seem to be aiming at us foreign devils. It's the other Chinese they want to intimidate. Otherwise they could drop them outside every European house. Easily. There are only Chinese living in that street where those two kids were killed.'

'But they could start doing that any time, leaving them outside European houses.'

'Then I'd be worried all right.'

They both watched the blue and black stack of a Blue Funnel cargo-boat moving slowly past the stern of the ferry. They had sailed with a Blue Funnel ship when Helen had first come to Hong Kong with him. And often afterwards they used to wander down to the harbour together to watch the Blue Funnel ships unloading. Many years now since they had done that together, or anything else for that matter, except as a duty to the children.

'You seem as depressed as I usually am.' Helen resumed, again half-accusingly.

'Do I? What's it like to live with?'

She took that in silence at first, then sighed with exasperated dejection. 'If we're going to go on like this on our leave, we'd better go separately. We'd both be better off. What's the point of us being together?'

'What's the point of anything?' He shrugged. 'Why doesn't Elena go back to her ballet lessons, by the way?'

'Do you want her to pick up a bomb?'

He turned. 'Well, let's get back in the car after that invigorating breath of sea air and bitchiness.'

The ferry was nosing into its jetty beneath the tenement blocks of Yaumati. The morning sunlight blazed dazzlingly on the rows of waiting cars and glinted on their windscreens. How is it possible to hate one's life so much, and still go on? Dimitri wondered, for the hundredth futile time.

'Aren't you going to have a swim?'

'Presently.'

'Why on earth do you drive here in the boiling sun if you're not even going to have a swim?'

'I will have a swim presently, I said. I suppose I can please myself about when I actually go in, can't I?'

She gave a short, angry sigh, got up and walked towards the sea. He was lying on his front, feeling the heat of the sun pricking his back. He lifted his head to watch her. She was fastening the strap of her white bathing cap as she walked and he could see her frowning impatiently because the catch would not fasten. When she reached the sea, she waded out to her knees and stood for a long time, arms folded, gazing down at the water as if she had forgotten why she had come there. The children were swimming towards her, calling her, but she was too deeply immersed in her brooding to hear them.

She's got good reason to hate me, he thought. I'm so sour and bitter these days. When she surfaces, I plunge. And *vice versa*. He lay down again, returning to his own brooding.

'When shall I see you again, Dimitri — Shall I see you again?' There had been a calm challenge in Mila's voice when they parted outside the police station.

'I don't know,' he had not been sure which of her questions he was answering. 'I'll give you a ring.'

'All right. Tsoi-geen.' She raised her hand and waved it gently sideways.

'Tsoi-geen.'

It seemed like *adieu*, not *au revoir*.

But he had not phoned her, and it was more than a month now. East is east and west is west, the absurd cliche kept running through his head while the sun scorched his neck and he stubbornly refused to move his head to the shade. East is east and west is west. He grasped two handfuls of dry, hot sand and let them sift through his fingers.

He said that someone was being beaten up. But I did not notice anything.

The waves thumping gently on the shore made the beach throb faintly under his ear. The cries of children in the water, the ineluctable blare of transistor radios, far enough away now to be soothing, the fat, newspaper-reading European man bulging over a canvas stool under a striped beach umbrella, the recurring pulse of the surf on the shore.

Twenty miles away the Chinese army masses and watches and the scattered Gurkhas watch them watching and nobody knows what will happen next, when the next bomb will be thrown, the next shot fired, and east is east and west is west and we lie on the beach as if everything was always going to be the same.

I did not notice anything.

When shall I see you again?

And the image of her floated in his mind once more, the way she had of brushing the hair away from her eyes, one hand each side of her face, her finger-tips just lifting and then stroking it back behind her ears with a ripple of her wrists. And then, arms poised, clasping the hair tight on the nape of her neck, pulling it sleekly over her small round head — Why is it just that gesture that I can't forget?

Someone was shouting further along the beach. Then all at once the life-guards were ringing their bells and everyone seemed to be shouting and running together, bare feet kicking up the sand. Dimitri looked anxiously for the children, fearing sharks or drowning. The sea was emptying, every swimmer threshing in towards the beach. A jabbering crowd had formed where the first shouts had come from.

He couldn't see Helen or the children. He ran to the crowd and pushed past the small brown Cantonese and the large white Europeans. His heart stopped pounding as he saw Helen standing with the children near the middle of the crowd. She was trying to pull them away, but they were staring resistingly at something wallowing amongst the rocks in the shallow water. Dimitri could see easily past the smaller Cantonese. At first he thought it was a large dead fish, then a sack, and then he saw it was a bloated, rotting human corpse.

The crowd was silent now, jostling only at the edges. They were all staring fascinated at the putrescent greenish flesh, tilting and bumping against the rocks as the waves broke and washed in. It lay face down. The arms were fastened with wire behind the back. All round the wire, the flesh had rotted away to the bone. The few Europeans watched with noses wrinkled in horror. The many Chinese were either expressionless or giggling behind their hands, though not in amusement. Dimitri saw the mixture of fascination and repulsion in Alex's and Elena's eyes. Suddenly they stopped resisting and let Helen pull them away.

Dimitri followed. Helen began collecting up the towels and putting them neatly in the beach basket. Elena stood silently watching her.

'What happened, Dimitri?' Alexander asked. 'Was it a man or a woman?'

He put his hand on Elena's shoulder. She was shivering. 'I couldn't tell, Alex — I didn't notice.'

It was not until they were in the car that he realised that Helen too was shivering. Her face had gone grey and her lips were trembling loosely.

She leant back and closed her eyes. Then suddenly she started screaming. 'I want to go back! I want to go back! I want to go back!' She began rocking to and fro, hammering on the dashboard with her fists as her shrieks became shriller and shriller. 'Don't you understand? I want to go back!' But she was not crying. Her eyes were quite dry. The children gazed at her with a new startled incomprehension and alarm. It was the first time they had seen her break down.

'I want to go back, Dimitri! I want to go back!'

'All right, Helen, all right.'

'I want to go back, don't you understand? I want to go back! Back! Back! Back!.' And then she began to cry at last, her lips writhing and slobbery, quivering in helpless spasms.

BRITISH MISSION IN PEKING SACKED

Thousand of Red Guards yesterday broke into the British Mission in Peking, ransacked the building and set it on fire. The twenty-three occupants of the building, of whom five were women, were subjected to a screaming barrage of abuse. The men were all kicked and beaten and had to be rescued by troops of the People's Liberation Army who, together with police, had until the last moment made no attempt to control the rampaging mob. It is understood that the Mission is completely destroyed.

The attack, which came at the expiry of China's forty-eight-hour ultimatum for the release of communist journalists imprisoned in Hong Kong, took place while the mission staff were sheltering in an inner office, watching a comedy film. The screaming mob smashed through the gates and surged into the compound, shouting 'Death! Death! and breaking up everything in sight. Petrol cans were thrown in the garden and along the walls and before long the whole mission was ablaze. When the staff were on the point of being overcome by smoke and the building was in danger of collapsing, they began to leave in an orderly manner. It was then that the mob attacked them.

Shock and dismay were expressed throughout the world at this flagrant contravention of accepted codes of diplomatic behaviour. Some quarters also expressed fears for the safety of Mr Antony Grey, the Reuter's correspondent who has been under house arrest without trial since July 21st in retaliation for the arrest of left-wing journalists in Hong Kong.

'Have some coffee, Jan.'

'No thanks.' Jan looked bulkily uncomfortable in his police uniform. 'I can't stay ... I just dropped by with this parcel. Lisa asked me to give it to Helen.'

'Oh. She's not back yet.'

Jan grunted. He laid his stiff blue cap in the table and turned to the window, still holding the parcel in his hands.

How absurd men look in shorts, Dimitri thought, gazing at the back of Jan's knees beneath the stiff, wide khaki shorts. Below the knees his heavy calves were covered with blue-bordered officer's socks leading down to heavy black shoes.

'I don't know what it iss.' Jan spoke draggingly, staring out of the window at the ground eleven floors below. 'I think it iss a record or something.'

'Looks like it. As long as it's not a bomb.'

Jan glanced back at him without smiling, put the parcel down beside his hat, then slowly turned away again. He leaned heavily on the bare teak window-sill, warped and discoloured by years of typhoon rains and burning suns. Thiss case of yours, Dimitri ...' He was feeling for words. 'You know there might be somm difficulties ...'

'Oh?'

'For you, I mean.'

Dimitri's eyes focused on the creased skin of Jan's neck above his starched khaki collar. 'How?' His voice tautened.

Jan was still staring down through the window, as if absorbed in whatever was happening on the ground below. 'Well, there might be somm people who will try to pay you back.'

'For making a statement?'

He nodded. 'They might try to get at you in any way they can.'

'Who? In the police?'

'You know Hong Kong.'

'Meaning?' A hostile gap seemed suddenly to have opened between them. Dimitri's voice was tauter and colder.

'You know Hong Kong,' Jan said again. 'There are bound to be somm people who ... resent.'

'So?' His gaze shifted to the short grey hair at the back of Jan's head then down to the creased skin of his thick neck again. It occurred to him that Jan's neck was in fact fat and ugly. 'So they resent it?'

Jan shrugged. 'I comm to say, be careful.'

'Of what?'

Jan lifted his hands and let them drop abruptly on to the window sill again. 'Dimitri, you know Hong Kong,' he spoke reprovingly. 'You do not need to be told how it iss done.'

'Are you trying to warn me off being a witness?'

'I am trying to warn you, not warn you off.'

'Who sent you?'

'That wass not necessary, Dimitri.' His voice too had an edge on it now. He turned and looked rigidly at Dimitri for some seconds with his very pale blue eyes that were almost grey. 'I am not sent by anyone. I comm myself.'

'I'm sorry, Jan.'

Jan took his cap from the table and brushed the nap with the back of his hand. A gesture that Dimitri must have seen a hundred times, this time it seemed to have a decisive finality about it. 'I shall be gone next month, they have no more use for me. If they want to send someone it will not be me.'

'I'm sorry, Jan,' he said again, not quite believingly.

Jan was nodding with unspoken thoughts as he walked heavily to the door. 'Like my Alsatian.' He turned, putting on his cap. 'You remember him? When we lived next to a Chinese banker and he had a Chow? The dogs had a big fight and that Chow got hurt. You remember? He did not come and talk to me, he never complained to me, that man ... But one day my Alsatian died with strychnine in his food.' He straightened his back and drew back his shoulders. The peak of his cap was sternly straight over his eyes. 'You know Hong Kong. It will be done like that, to get at you ... They do not send me. I came by myself.' He opened the door and went out, still nodding.

Dimitri went to the window where Jan had been standing. Below was a police Landrover, parked in the long shade of the block of flats. The driver was leaning against the bonnet. He stiffened and saluted. Jan climbed in and the Landrover drove slowly away.

On the little patch of concrete outside the caretaker's room, several amahs were gathered round the old fish-woman from Aberdeen. The fish-woman's hoarse cries echoed off the back of the building. The amahs chattered shrilly. He saw Ah Wong there, older and aloof from the rest. The fish-woman had a snake to sell today, a long, black sinuous thing which she pulled out of a basket and lifted up by the throat. It wriggled and writhed helplessly. Like a man hanging, he thought suddenly. The fish-woman took a knife from the ground beside her and, still shouting her cries off the back of the building, began skinning the snake alive. The snake jumped and twisted as if it were screaming in silent pain and the amahs bargained shrilly with the fish-woman while a dark pool of blood spread out at her feet. When she had pulled the skin off, she began cutting. And the amahs took pieces of the snake away in little clear plastic bags.

The fish-woman's face was brown and impassive. She wiped her knife on her dirty drab-blue trousers, counted the money, then started chopping again. For some reason her face reminded him of an old man he had seen sleeping on the street in Aberdeen one winter, spitting greenish phlegm on to the pavement beneath a tattered, wind-flapped coca-cola advertisement. And of an old woman outside the hospital, who had met his eyes as she was being helped on to the bus by her two daughters. She had looked at him with eyes deepened by pain and the look had made him uneasy, guilty, as if she had been blaming him for her suffering. Years ago. Now both of them must be dead.

You know Hong Kong.

He stared still at the fish-woman still chopping and slicing the white flesh of the snake. When he heard Helen's key in the door he did not turn.

'Are you still here? Don't you have to go to the university today?'

'Yes. Later.'

'What's this?' She picked up the parcel.

'Jan brought it. He's just gone.'

She tore at the paper. 'It's that record we lent them years ago. How exact Lisa is. She sighed and sat down. 'What's the matter with you?'

'Nothing.'

'What are you staring at then? Do I *have* to talk to your back?'

'I'm watching the fish-woman killing a snake.'

Burr-burr ... Burr-burr ... Burr-burr ... Burr-burr ... Burr-burr ... Burr
—

Silence.
'Mila'?
'Dimitri.'
Silence.
'Mila, you always do that, did you know?'
'Do what?'
'You pick up the phone and you don't answer. You always wait for the other person to speak first.'
'It is because they are calling me, so they must have something to say.'
'Oh.'
Silence.
'Well I said I'd give you a ring.'
'But you did not mean it when you said it.'
'I don't know. But ...anyway, it looks as though you were right. About the consequences of making a statement, I mean.'
'What has happened?'
'Nothing, yet. But Jan warned me something might.'
Silence.
'Mila?'
'I was thinking about it.'
'Can I see you? Did you know your voice is very low on the phone?'
'This afternoon I am teaching.'
'Till when?'
'Till eight.'
'I'll pick you up at quarter past?'
'All right.'
'Mila, it feels so strange on the phone.'
'Yes, doesn't it?'
'But I've wanted to phone you lots of times.'
'Yes, I know.'
'Yes, you know? How?'
'Because I have wanted to phone you too.'
'What have you been doing all this time?'
'I read a lot. It is only twenty-seven and a half days.'
'What? What have you been reading?'
'A lot of sad Chinese poems that made me feel sorry for myself.'

'They didn't make you feel harmonious?'
'Yes, they made me harmonious too.'

'I brought this for you.'
    'What? A rose? Is that for starting again or … ?'
    'For starting again. Your hair looks awful.'
    'You never like pigtails. Where are we going?'
    'To Turtle Cove.'
    'Turtle Cove? Why?'
    'Because I want to take you to Turtle Cove.'
    'Is not the curfew on there?'
    'No, only in Kowloon tonight.'
    'I have brought something for you too.'
    'What is it? A scroll?'
    'My own bad calligraphy. Do you know this poem?'
    'No wonder you've been sad if you've been reading that.'
    'It is sad and it is not sad — both together.'
    'I'll lock it up in my room at the university and keep peeping at it
as if it was a dirty postcard.'

It was dark already when they reached the beach. Dimitri parked the
car off the road and they started walking down the steep path under
the trees. Mila carried her rose. They had scarcely talked in the car as
they drove along the narrow road past the police check points and the
fishing boats at Aberdeen. There had been the suspense of
unfamiliarity between them. But now as they walked, Mila untied the
ribbons in her hair and shook it free.
    'That's better,' he caught her hand.
    'I used to come here on school outings.'
    'Which school did you go to?'
    'One of the nuns' schools. I had to leave because they would not let
me go to ballet lessons. They thought it was indecent.'
    The path opened suddenly on to the narrow, empty beach, set back
between two steep headlands. There was no moon; the sand looked
grey, the sea smooth and black. A junk was moving far out across the
bay, a single yellow light on its mast. The dark shape of its sail drifted
very slowly across the paler darkness of the sky.
    They walked along to the far end of the beach, kicking up the
sand. Dimitri was sweating. The air had the sultry heaviness that
comes before typhoons.

'Is there a typhoon coming?'

'I don't know. What did your friend Jan say?'

'First we are going to have a swim.'

'Aiya, I have no costume.'

'First we are going to have a swim.'

But it was she who raced into the water first, kicking up a brilliant shower of phosphorescent spray. He ran after her, but she was a better swimmer. Whenever he tried to catch an arm or leg she slipped away easily, kicking a shower of salty water into his face. But as she climbed out, wet hair streaming down her back, she lost her footing on the steeply shelving beach and he caught her as she wobbled and struggled against the tug of the backward washing waves. They were trembling with eagerness and tumbled down where they were, half in the water, half on the sand.

He opened his eyes as he slipped out of her. Her hair was drifting in the ebb and flow of the waves, fanning round her head like a veil.

He helped her up and they walked back to where their clothes lay.

'Now I have sand all over my head,' she said matter-of-factly. She picked up the rose and pushed it into the wet hair behind her ear. 'Tahiti, look at me. Tahiti.'

Their bodies dried slowly in the warm air. Somewhere up the hill a dog was howling. The junk had passed behind the dense black mass of the headland. Mila laid her head on his belly and he fingered the velvety petals of the rose by her ear. She turned her eyes up to him.

'What did your friend Jan say?'

'That somebody might try to get at me. But not directly.'

She looked back at the sea. 'It is the way. I told you.'

He gazed down the length of her body. Little rivulets of water trickled down her skin into the sand, gleaming faintly in the dim light of the stars. 'How will they try to do it?'

'Helen or me.'

'Meaning?'

She did not answer at first but then she shrugged. 'I have been told I will be all right if I do not change my story.'

'They've got at you?'

'Oh yes. What did you think?'

'Who?'

She shrugged again. 'A phone call, that is all.'

'We should go to the Anti-Corruption Branch.'

'There is no proof. Besides, I will not go. And your friend Jan will deny it if you tell them about him.'

'How do you know?'

'Otherwise he would have gone to them himself, wouldn't he?'

He grasped a handful of sand and let it sift through his fingers on to her navel.

'Everyone has something to hide,' she raised her head to blow at the sand, then turned to look at him. 'Perhaps they will try Helen.'

'How?' He picked up another handful, frowning. 'She's taking the kids away on leave next month. They'll be gone for four months. The trial'll be over by then.'

'Ah.' She let her head down again. 'And you? 'she asked quietly.

'I'll stay. I have this book to finish, and the trial ... Helen's just about on the edge. She can't take any more ... We saw one of those corpses at the beach last week. She broke up. It's affecting the kids too, of course.' He was letting the sand sift on to her breasts now, first one nipple, then the other.

'Helen is affecting them?'

'Everything is. You and me, Helen, the kids.'

'But they do not know about us?'

'They feel the antagonism between Helen and me has got worse and it's worse since I've known you.'

'I'm sorry.'

'No, you shouldn't be sorry. It was worst of all these past weeks when I didn't see you at all. Let's go to Macau for a bit, after Helen's gone. We would have a week without anything hanging over us. There wouldn't even be any bombs.'

She turned on to her front and propped herself on her elbows, letting her hair hang down till it just brushed the skin of his belly. 'Won't you miss your children for four months?'

He cupped his hand round her head. 'Not if I have you.'

'That is sad.'

'Why?' He forced her head gently down.

She kissed him and then stroked the hair of his chest and belly with her cheek. 'Because it is exclusive.'

'*Aiya!*' He jumped and cursed in Cantonese.

'What's wrong?' she too spoke in Cantonese.

'You've just dug a trench in me with a thorn from your damned rose!'

She looked down and smiled. There was a thin dark scratch along his belly, with several pricks of blood spurting along it. Lowering her head again, she licked the blood up with her tongue.

I get up in the morning and I'm tired and I want to go on sleeping, but I know I can't. I know the whole day will go in heat and shopping and fighting with the amah and controlling the children until ten at night, and then there is a blank gap while I sleep and it starts again, eternally the same. And everything I do I hate. I wasn't made for this, but there's no escape.

Their language, I can't speak their language after all these years. They laugh at me in the markets. They cheat me into my face. The amah despises me. And I am locked up in it, I can't get away. Dimitri can talk to them, be was born here, but I am always a stranger, always resented.

And now the bombs and the riots, that's the last thing. I can't take it any more, I can feel myself sinking, fading. Heat, dirt, cheating, squabbling children, sullen amah and nothing of what I want to do. I can't go on. And now bombs. And bodies floating in the sea. And all they did was giggle. It was a human being, one of theirs, even. And all they could do was giggle. I can't any more, I can't. I wish I could just walk away and never see any of it again.

Reminder — Examination Failures Committee,
10 a.m. Dean's office

The other members of the committee were already there, Frank Browning, Sarah Misson the Dean, and C. K. Tsong.

'Sorry if I'm late.'

'Not at all, Dimitri.' Sarah waved and spoke with her habitual exuberant cheerfulness. 'We're early, just having a natter.'

He sat down in the empty chair she had waved him to, glancing through the tall windows at the azaleas flowering outside. A large air-conditioner rattled noisily, but although the air was cool, it reeked of the smoke from Frank's cigar.

'... wondering about maturity,' Frank was saying. 'I mean, does pubic hair grow on Chinese girls as early as it does on Europeans, C.K.?'

C.K.'s eyes were hooded. He blushed beneath his pale almond skin and fingered a strangely. old-fashioned pearl tie-pin, affecting not to have heard Frank.

Sarah, who was not in the least embarrassed by the question itself, was clearly embarrassed at its being put to C.K. She fussed with the papers in front of her and shook her head, twitching the short, blue-rinsed curls of her unmistakably grey hair.

But Frank was impervious to atmosphere — or pretended he was. He pursued C. K with a superb indifference even to the actual facial wrigglings, which expressed his embarrassment and displeasure. 'I mean, most of our students seem to mature in different ways from European students and I was wondering about physical signs of puberty. I would have thought, that physically they matured faster, you know. Some of those bar-girls in Wanchai are only twelve or thirteen, I'm told. Positive nymphettes, I mean… What's your observation been, C.K.?'

C.K.'s quick brown eyes flickered helplessly at Sarah and Dimitri, like a child interrogated by his teacher in front of his parents. His skin turned blotchy with the rising blood beneath. At last he giggled, covering his mouth with his hand, the ultimate gesture of embarrassment.

'Er, hadn't we better have a word about the appellants?' Sarah managed to deflect Frank from further pursuit. 'It's nearly time to see the first one.'

Dimitri wondered, as he flicked through the papers in his file, whether Frank really was impervious to the atmosphere he had created, or whether he was rather out to enhance the reputation he enjoyed as an eccentric. That bluff innocence could not be entirely ingenuous. If he had not embarrassed C.K. deliberately, he must surely have noticed that he *was* embarrassed and then deliberately done nothing about it. That suggested Frank was really a missionary of the common-sense school, a homespun philosopher of the plain word. An Englishman would perhaps have recognised this easily and could have known how to deal with him. But how did C.K. see him? C.K.'s father had taken the Mandarin examination and entered the imperial civil service in 1909, while C.K. himself had been educated first in Shanghai and then at Harvard. Did he perceive Frank through wholly traditional eyes as a coarse, blundering foreign devil? ('She sat on the floor!' one of Dimitri's girl students had said in amazed contempt about an American undergraduate visiting the university.) Or was his perception at least partially modified by his Western education, so that he would assess Frank's actions in the way Dimitri himself had just done? The deprecatory giggle and blush, the refusal to answer — or even, apparently, to comprehend — Frank's question made it obvious enough that C. K.'s reaction was the traditional one. More than embarrassment for himself, of course, his behaviour was an indication of displeasure which a Chinese would have understood to be a severe rebuke. But such delicate nuances were beyond Frank's ken, if they were not beneath it. Gibbon's apothegm about history would need some amendment in the context of China and the West, Dimitri smiled to himself. History here was in truth little more than the register of the misunderstandings of mankind. That had been confirmed even with Mila in the business of their statements to the police.

'What do you think, Dimitri?' Sarah's booming cheerfulness shattered this fragile chain of reflections. She was discussing the merits of the three appellants' cases. One of them, a girl, had claimed financial hardship as the reason for her failure. The other two cited 'personal troubles' and one was supported by a psychiatrist's report. All of them asked to be allowed to stay in the university and sit the examination again next year.

He shrugged. 'Let's see them.'

'Yes. Shall we have the first one in now?'

She was a shy, diminutive girl with narrow hands, which she kept clasping and reclasping in her lap. Her face looked harrowed, near to tears.

'I'm sorry to see you in this situation,' Sarah's voice just missed a tone of patronising bonhomie by virtue of its evident warmth. 'Now we've read all the documents here, but is there anything else you'd like to tell us about?'

The girl sat in front of them, blinking behind her thick-lensed glasses, and spoke in halting English about her family troubles. Her parents had not wanted her to go to university because it would delay the time when she could start earning money for them, although, since she would be supported by a government bursary, she would not cost them much while she studied. Eventually, they had given their consent, provided she gave them five hundred dollars a month. She had found this by giving English lessons for four hours every day, with the predictable result that she had failed her examination in two papers.

She told her story, one of a kind long familiar to all of them, with a shame-faced expression as if she were somehow to blame for her difficulties. When she had finished, she sat still, hanging her head. She was plain and submissive, neatly but dowdily dressed.

'If you are given another chance, will you be able to pass the examination, do you think?'

'Yes.'

'But will you carry on giving all these lessons?'

'I must give money to my parents.'

Sarah looked at C.K. He kept shuffling his papers and bending down the corners while he talked to her.

'What does your father do?'

'He is a clerk.'

'So he has about five hundred dollars a month?'

'Yes.' She blushed to admit so small a salary.

'You live in a resettlement estate?'

'In Wong Tai Sin, yes.'

'So there have been many riots there recently?'

'Yes. Quite many.'

'And bombs?'

'Not too much bombs.'

'In Wong Tai Sin, how many rooms does your family have?'

'One room and a kitchen.'

'And how many in your family?'

'Eight.'

If C.K. hoped to shame his European colleagues by persisting in this interrogation, he was succeeding. None of them could survive on five hundred dollars a month in the cement squalor of a resettlement estate. And the way they were fidgeting silently with their papers showed that they knew it. Yet it wasn't clear that the accusing finger should point only at the Europeans, Dimitri reflected. The Colony's *laissez faire* approach to the welfare of its people had been as much the fault of the rich Chinese as of an apathetic administrative bureaucracy. Many of the many Chinese millionaires in Hong Kong exemplified the ultimate ruthless degeneracy of Confucianism, leaving all outside their own families to live or die as fortune ordained. While workers generally had to work long hours for low pay, it was nearly always a Chinese firm which worked them longest and for least. 'Some people eat in the Hilton, some people eat in the street,' a Chinese employer had said in court, when the magistrate asked him whether the salary of seventy-five dollars a month he paid to one of his workers would give him enough to eat. Such men were often powerful, perhaps all-powerful, advisers of the government. Would the riots and bombs change any of this? The campaign seemed to be led by ideological fanatics, more interested in *who* ruled than how.

It was his turn to question the girl.

'What do you want to do when you've got your degree, if you're allowed to continue?'

'I wish to go abroad and further my studies.'

'Where?'

'In America.'

The old dream that had enticed poor Hungarians, Poles, Irish, Russians and Jews to America a hundred years -ago was still powerful in Hong Kong. Dimitri had rarely known a student who did not have America written on his heart. They studied here only to get out. And yet those few that reached America — did their dream come as true as they had hoped? He thought of his own application to London. Would that in the end make any difference? The wells of happiness are seldom found where everybody digs and drills. Or, if found, they often soon run dry.

'Oil doesn't always gush where the prospector drills,' he spoke drily, half to himself.

The girl gazed at him nonplussed and almost alarmed.

'Never mind,' he reassured her in Cantonese. 'It doesn't matter.'

'We ought to give her another bash at it,' Frank said when she left. 'She might scrape through.'

They all nodded silently, perhaps guiltily. The girl's future was really bleakly clear to them all. If she did scrape through her examination at last, she would never go further and would probably end up as a timid, conscientious secondary-school teacher, helping to support her family until she was married off and forgot her dreams of America. Long dead hours of routine instructions from a jaded syllabus to dutiful children, who would obediently learn their lessons, get into the university and repeat the process all over again. Only *her* pupils might find themselves greeting the soldiers of the PLA, if not in the next five years, at least in the next twenty. They would hardly have been prepared for the change, but they would endure it as they endured everything that was imposed by authority.

The second applicant looked both furtive and sullen. He seemed undecided whether to sidle or swagger into the room and so compromised by doing each in turn. His application, written in the Chinglish which Dimitri no longer even noticed, was a similar injudicious blend of veiled resentment at the examiners' failure to pass him and plaintive entreaty for the committee's sympathy in his 'dejected situation.' The resentment seemed to be tenuously connected with a vague anti-colonialism and, its concomitant, absurd chauvinism. Reading the letter again while Sarah and Frank questioned the man, Dimitri sensed the only just unspoken thought that his failure was somehow an instance of colonial oppression. Dimitri wondered how sympathetic C.K. would be to this attitude.

C.K. soon settled that when he began asking the man about his attendance. Apparently he had scarcely been seen by his tutor during the whole of the year. When C.K. asked him why, he merely shook his head, suddenly abashed.

'Did you have to work to support yourself?'

'No.' A slight curl of the lip at the very idea.

'Why do you think you should be given another chance, then?' The polite smile and soft voice in which C.K. put these questions did nothing to disguise his impatience. Clearly lazy students offended more than cloudy anti-colonialism pleased him, if indeed it pleased him at all.

'Well, my father will retire soon and he will not be able to bear if I do not succeed to have a degree.'

'Perhaps it would have been better to consider that earlier?' C.K. smiled gently at him.

Sarah began again, but Dimitri stopped listening. Helen and the children were leaving that afternoon and he felt himself withdrawing from this public, social world into the private and silent intimacy of his mind. There was a tacit uncertainty between Helen and himself about whether she would return after her three months' leave. Their chill alienation from each other had recently been turning into hostility and bitterness. How would they go on? No doubt the change was partly due to Mila. A prisoner chafes more if he sees open fields through the bars than if he has no view of freedom whatsoever.

The man left at last and the three of them went on discussing him, although their minds were already made up. Dimitri watched them detachedly, through the perspectives of his inner space. C.K.'s lips quivered slightly when he talked. The skin under his chin was loose and hanging. Frank was laughing as he knocked the ash off his cigar, Sarah laughing too, pushing her glasses higher up her nose. Dimitri's eyes focused abstractedly on C.K.'s pearl tie-pin, moving up and down on his grey silk tie as he breathed. What are these antics we are performing? he thought, not for the first time. What is this charade we pretend to be absorbed in? How absurd to bother with all this! What inanity! The movement of a pearl on a grey tie over a white shirt above an ageing human skin, wrinkled but hairless, that is the reality. Everything else is just an elaborate game of make-believe.

The last applicant was the one whose appeal was supported by a psychiatrist's report. He had been being treated for depression for some months and had failed the examination badly. The psychiatrist wrote that he was responding to treatment and should be able to attend to his work if he were given another chance. At the same time there was a hint that if his appeal was rejected he might relapse into the depression which he was only just laboriously emerging from.

'Neurosis' affected Sarah powerfully. People with her bluff, warm character were usually unable to appreciate what those they called neurotic actually experienced. And so they were often more sympathetic than fellow-melancholics might have been, because the manifestations of withdrawal were more disturbing to them. Those to whom the remote depths were familiar knew that they were also a certain refuge.

The man came in with a reserved and preoccupied look in his eyes, as if he could not quite bring himself to attend fully because his thoughts lingered on something more absorbing. But he smiled with ironic appreciation when Sarah began feeling for questions that would allude tactfully to his illness without mentioning it.

'They *tell* me I am getting better,' he said, as if he at least was not quite convinced. 'I am able to work sometimes now. Before the examination I am not able to work at all. I just sit and...' He ended with a helpless shrug and a melancholy smile of apology.

'Well, what did you do all day?'

Although he smiled as he shook his head, his eyes still held the dulled, abstracted look Dimitri had first noticed. 'Nothing. I was just ... brooding?' He looked up questioningly, to see if he had found the right word.

'Brooding?' Frank made it sound vaguely obscene, as if he had said 'masturbating.' 'Brooding? What about? Your work? Girlfriend?'

'No, my family. They are still in mainland.'

'Oh.' He nibbled his cigar unsurely.

'I did not hear from them for a long time… Then the bodies in the sea… The last time they wrote, they said… they asked my aunt not to send any more money because it is dangerous for them.' Again his apologetic, self-deprecating smile. 'So I sit and think…'

'I see …' Frank's voice had lost its slightly hectoring tone. He tapped the ash off his cigar, frowning. Dimitri wondered how many students concealed a similar history behind that reserved, watchful look in their eyes which was so easily mistaken for bland impassivity. He remembered Edwin Fung, whose father had been imprisoned for being a landlord. Edwin's family dared not write to him and dared not return. His mother, who had been sent to Hong Kong before the communist takeover, had lived the life of a widow for fifteen years. Edwin, like this man, seemed to regard these misfortunes as part of the normal course of human existence, scarcely to be remarked upon. Certainly, they felt no bitterness or hostility to the communist rulers. Edwin, for instance, acknowledged that his eyes pricked with emotion when he went to see the propaganda films shown by communist cinemas — propaganda of the crudest kind, which he would have ridiculed if it had been produced by an American agency. The miseries and injustices — to Western eyes — which their families suffered were regarded by these Chinese more as if they were acts of God, to whose status indeed the rulers of China had for centuries successfully aspired. They were to be expected, avoided if possible and otherwise accepted, inevitable consequents of the things done by the new rulers, which had restored China to order and peace within and power and respect outside. This change they admired with pride, but from a distance.

'What do you want to do when — if — you get a degree?' he asked suddenly.

'To further my studies abroad, in America.'

Sarah shook her blue-rinsed curls again as the door closed on him. 'What an extraordinary university this is … Half of the students are school-teachers while they're working for a degree, half of them are refugees and all of them want to go to America of all places …' Once she had travelled through America on her way back to England and ever since she had considered it a special kind of hell made up entirely of five-lane throughways and neon-lit Howard Johnsons. 'And yet we go on behaving as if we were in a provincial British university.'

'Well, how else should we behave?' Frank asked innocently.

'Mm? Well, anyway, I suppose we'll wait for him to get better and then give him another chance? Is that all right?'

C.K. left at once, with a politely aloof smile. He was never quite comfortable with Europeans, particularly when they expressed themselves freely or, which was the same thing, ignorantly about Hong Kong and China.

'I wonder sometimes about us pink-faced devils sitting in judgement over these students like that ...' Dimitri continued aloud the thoughts which had silently accompanied C.K.'s departure.

'Why?' Sarah bristled. 'I treat them just the same as I would any student.'

'Well, you were just saying how absurd it was for us to treat this place as if it was a British provincial university. How much more absurd it must seem to them. I mean, why should they do things our way rather than us do things their way?'

'There's no our way or their way, there's only a right way and a wrong way!'

'Dimitri, if you're suggesting we should all resign and go home, the answer is I can't afford it.' Frank chuckled, examining the wet, chewed end of his cigar. "Too well paid here, you know. Can't afford to resign. Unless they bomb me out, of course. Which it looks as though they may do yet.'

'I suppose I think we really ought not to be here at all,' Dimitri said feebly, already withdrawing again into his thoughts.

'Oh well, everyone thinks that. Time for a beer. I hear they found some bombs by the library last night by the way. Is that true? Burn the books now, eh? Soon it'll be burn the bookworms.'

RADIO ANNOUNCER ASSASSINATED
TERRORIST AMBUSH IN KOWLOON

Mr Lam Bun, thirty-seven-year-old popular Commercial Radio announcer, died in Queen Elizabeth Hospital today after the car in which he was travelling to work with his cousin was set on fire with petrol bombs by three communist agitators.

Mr Lam, who was noted for his fearless condemnation of leftist troublemakers, had just driven into Man Wei Road when three men disguised as road workers held up a red flag in front of him. As he stopped, one of the men threw a petrol bomb into the car, which immediately burst into flames. The two occupants staggered out, badly burned. Their assailants threw petrol over them and set them on fire, running off while the two victims writhed on the ground.

Mr Lam had been threatened anonymously with bodily harm if he persisted in his condemnation of the communists. He managed to tell the first person to come to his aid that he and his cousin had been attacked by communist agitators before collapsing unconscious like his cousin. Mr Lam recovered consciousness briefly during a visit from his wife today, but died shortly after she had left his bedside. His cousin, Mr Lam Kwong-Hoi, has not recovered consciousness yet. A spokesman for the hospital described his condition as, very critical'.

It was reported unofficially that Mr Lam's name was on a communist execution list which is being passed round leftist groups in mimeographed form. Other prominent opponents of the agitators are said to be on the list, including some highly placed Chinese officials in the government. However the police were unable to confirm or deny the existence of such a list. When asked whether any prominent citizens were being given police protection, the police spokesman said, 'We always take certain precautions, but it would not be advisable to say exactly what they are.'

It is understood that an award will be offered for the arrest and conviction of Mr Lam's killers. His body will lie in the Kowloon Funeral Parlour all day on Wednesday, to enable his many fans to pay their last respects and tributes before the funeral on Thursday.

Dimitri and Mila leant over the taffrail of the little *Tai Loy*. The light of the setting sun glowed on the receding white concrete skyscrapers of Victoria and Kennedy Town. The ship shuddered gently as the engines went to full speed and the propellers churned the sea beneath them. The sun sank lower with each minute and the pink glow retreated inch by inch up the skyscrapers, leaving the lower parts grey and indistinct in dusk and distance.

Behind them, in the tiny saloon, the inevitable Mah Jong tiles clacked and clattered. The sea was glassy-still, but a heavily jewelled Chinese lady lay supine in a deck-chair, eyes closed, frowning, pale and with a crumpled handkerchief held to her mouth.

A hydrofoil slipped past, skimming the surface like some flying fish, its porthole windows a row of staring eyes. On their starboard bow, the dark mass of Lantau frowned over them, lightless and bare, the sea breaking in a faint luminous foam against its stern, dark rocks. The little dumb-bell island of Cheung Chau slid away on the other side. Junks were crowded together in the curve of its harbour, lights flickering in their high poops where the fishermen's families were eating their evening rice.

'Have you heard from Helen?' Mila asked, the first thing she had said since they had passed through the immigration shed in Hong Kong.

'This is one of the most beautiful sea-trips in the world.'

She glanced at him sideways, holding her hair back with her hand. 'Have you heard from Helen, Dimitri?'

'Um... let me think ... Have I heard from Helen? Mmm ... Oh yes, I have.'

'And how is she?'

He smiled down at the foaming, swirling wake. 'You know your voice reminds me of someone dropping little pebbles into a basket. Each word is a separate little thing with its own identity. It's the way you speak English.'

'You mean that I should not ask such questions?'

'I'm sure Confucius must have said somewhere that it's not fitting for a mistress to discuss her lover's wife with him.'

'It is because you feel guilty.'

His eyebrows lifted slightly while he considered that. 'Anyway,' he said at last, prevaricating, 'as a typical Chinese girl you shouldn't be interested in anything outside your own family.'

'If you were a typical Chinese man, I might be your concubine now and then I would be a legal part of your family.'

'You don't believe in women's lib?'

It was she now who evaded. 'Is that the evening star, look?'

'Yes. What a pity travel ads have reduced all this to just the Technicolor backdrop of a Pan-Am flight.'

'Your Tennyson was doing that long before there were any travel ads.'

'Do you read Tennyson?'

'I had to at school. "Sunset and evening star".'

'Actually,' he was still gazing up at the evening star, loneliest and coldest of stars, 'Helen says she doesn't want to come back, except for the children's sake. Apparently, they miss me, strange as it may seem...'

First the flashing beam from the lighthouse, then the faintly swinging mast-lamps of a fleet of fishing junks, then at last the strings and loops of lights that hung upon the little hills of Macau. They passed the outer harbour, dark and empty, its long, low wall sentinelled by lonely, glimmering beacons, and then the curving Praia Grande, lined with trees, through whose leaves the dim street lamps shone as if they had been draped there for a festival. They rounded the headland slowly and eased into the inner harbour. A communist gunboat stood off a little way, floodlights playing on a vast portrait of Chairman Mao fixed to its side. Communist junks, decked with red flags and large-character slogans, nestled next to the brilliantly lit floating casino. A drab Portuguese marine police launch was moored by the *Tai Loy's* berth and a police official, cap on back of head, shirt unbuttoned, watched Dimitri and Mila incuriously as he drank his coffee.

'I was brought here by my mother before the Japanese war...' Dimitri sniffed the air. 'Three years old. It's hardly changed a bit.'

'Do you remember it from when you were there?'

'No, but I went back after the war. Helen and I used to come quite often, until...'

They moved towards the gangway. The jewelled Chinese lady was in front of them, yawning while she opened her handbag. Glancing over her shoulder, Dimitri could see wads of hundred dollar bills stacked neatly inside. She would play them all at the floating casino and return to Hong Kong the next morning, probably without having moved a hundred yards from the ship.

As they went down the steep gangway Dimitri touched Mila's shoulder. 'See that church front, the ruined one?' He pointed up at the floodlit facade of Sao Paulo, all that was left from the fire of 1835. 'Let's go there after dinner.'

The whole facade has been called a sermon in stone. At the top is the Dove of the Holy Ghost, set amid

the sun, the moon and the stars ... In the second tier
stands a bronze Christ-Child, whose left hand once
carried the orb of Kingship, the rest of this tier being
largely devoted to the Passion ... On the next tier, the
Blessed Virgin is surrounded by six angels and a
seraph head ... Beyond this is Death, depicted by a
prostrate skeleton armed with a scythe, but pierced
by an arrow, and beside it the inscription in Chinese
'He who remembers death will be without sin'.

The tap-tap-tap of the bamboo blind, flapping languidly in the breeze
against the window frame ... He lifted himself slowly and looked down
at her. Her face looked pale in the faint starlight falling through the
window. Her eyes were large shadows, glistening as they caught the
light.

'What are you thinking?' He stroked her hair on the pillow.

'Not thinking. Watching.'

'What are you watching, then?'

'There is a tjik-tjak on the wall over there. He has been watching us
all the time.'

He lay back beside her, looking up at the little lizard. It was
motionless, high up near the ceiling. Suddenly it darted a few inches
and stopped still again, so quick that his eye could scarcely follow it.
'Bloody voyeur.' He pulled her on top of him. 'Wish he'd catch a few
of these damned mosquitoes.'

She bit the skin of his shoulder with a sort of tender fierceness, the
way a dog chews its master's hand.

'Did you like the church, what's left of it?' He was feeling the
hollow of her back just above the swell of her hips, realising there were
still new ways of touching her, that whether it was with his finger-tips
or the palm of his hand would make a difference, whether it was with
the very tips of his fingers or the curled back of his knuckles.

She answered through her teeth, still clenched on his skin. 'I like
the church, I like this room, I like your body, I like everything.'

'What a strange thing happiness is.' He was gazing still at the
motionless tjik-tjak.

'Why?'

The Rua da Felicidade, or Street of Happiness, once
famous and animated as a haunt of the sing-song

girls and prostitutes, was a particularly brilliant scene on the eve of the seventh day of the seventh month, the festival of the ox-herd and the spinning maid, with whom the girls identified themselves. Then all the 'sisters' would gather to offer fruit to these deities and burn the elaborate paper models of a bridge with two figures on it, representing the bridge by which they were supposed to meet each other.

'Because they have named a street after it, because of you, because of everything. Tomorrow we'll go swimming.'

The Praia Grande no longer offers the splendid vistas of fine buildings recorded by 19th century paintings of Macau. Reclamation has deprived the Bay of its broad sweep and the architectural standard has deteriorated. Nevertheless it still offers, especially in the relative coolness of evening, a delightfully tree-shaded promenade with fine views across waters studded with fishing junks to the Chinese islands beyond. But in the early morning you may also see, bobbing against the retaining wall, the body of some refugee drowned in an effort to reach Macau by swimming.

'What is this beach called?'

'Black Sand beach.'

'Yes, the sand is dark.'

'We used to come here nearly every summer. My mother shared a bungalow with Jan and Lisa. That one up there, it looks just the same. I never knew its name. It had 'Casa' something painted in big white letters over the door, but the rest had worn away.'

She sat with her legs straight, toes pointed in front of her, and bent slowly forward from her hips, hands stretched above her head. Slowly she went down till her forward-falling hair and then her forehead touched her knees while her hands lay on her toes.

'How long did it take you to learn to do that?'

'About five years. I am getting stiff.'

Dimitri picked up a sea-rotted bamboo stick and began drawing a big square round her in the sand.

'What are you doing?' She came up slowly, then swept down again, her arms long and slender with a waving motion like wings. Her whole body lay along her legs now, as if resting.

'Staking a claim.' He gouged her name in Chinese characters in the sand, and then his own. And then the date, and the hour, and the minute. The writing went round all four sides of the square. 'There now I have you.'

'Yes.' She craned her head to read it all. 'But I am inside and you are outside.'

'Then you can't escape.'

'Not till the tide comes in and smoothes it away.'

'The tide doesn't come this far.'

'Yes, it does. Look at the seaweed.'

'That tjik-tjak is still there, look, on the wall.'

'Is he?' Dimitri slid off her on to the rumpled sheets. 'Knows A good performance when he sees one ... We ought to charge him for admission, like they do in the Street of Happiness.'

'Do they even charge tjik-tjaks?'

'I wouldn't be surprised.'

'What a lot you know about Macau.'

'Yes. Quite a bit. D'you know there is a wonderful little theatre here? All velvet and gold like a Victorian theatre in London. Helen and I heard a fado singer there once. I suppose it was like being in Lisbon in 1850 ... You know that poem Auden wrote about Macau — "Nothing ever happens here", or something? But it does happen, only slower ... And they used to have other concerts as well. Not only fado singers ... I wonder if they still do...'

'Why does Helen not take up the piano again? Does she not like it any more?'

'She's abandoned it, as if it had cheated her. She never plays, even at home ... Perhaps she wants to kill it, so that she won't feel bitter about it. Damn!'

'What?'

'I forgot to unpack your scroll. I brought it along to hang up.'

And he scrambled out of the bed and rummaged on his knees through the travelling bag, while she, propped on her elbow, watched, the other hand covering her breast.

At last he found it and hung it from the coat-hook on the door. 'There, that makes this room really civilised.'

'But it is sad, you think,' her eyes scanned the familiar characters again.

Dead bushes, old tree, twilight crow,
Small bridge, flowing water, human dwelling,
Ancient road, west wind, lean horse,
Evening sun, west set
Broken-hearted man at world's edge.

'Sad? Oh yes, it's sad all right,' he answered slowly.

> Within the entrance to the Camoes Garden stands the Luis de Camoes Museum. The Museum (open 10 a.m. to 5p.m., 50 cents entrance fee) has a rather run-down appearance but is well-kept inside. The various rooms are visited in a fixed clock-wise order. The first displays proto-historic Chinese funerary terracottas and other pottery; the second, Chinese monochrome pottery, notably Chinese white and ox-blood ware from Kwantung; the third, an impressive collection of Kwantung polychrome ware of every period; the fourth a variety of bronze articles, notably Buddhas, incense burners and other cult objects, coinage, etc.; the fifth, Western style porcelain used by Macau dignitaries; the sixth, a collection of rolls of Chinese paintings; the seventh, a number of sedan chairs, formerly used by ecclesiastical dignitaries and perfectly restored; the eighth, a fine assortment of sacred objects — vestments, paintings, wood-carvings and antiphonaries; the ninth and last, a gallery of water-colour views of Macau done during World War II by a Russian refugee called Smirnoff, with some works by Chinnery and other artists.

Mila stretched and sighed beside him. He watched the rippling swell of her breasts as her arms lifted, tensed and then released.
'Where are you taking me tomorrow, my furry beast?'
'To the old Protestant Cemetery.'

She lay on her side, head pillowed on her arm, gazing at him with the grave eyes and half-smiling lips that always made him uncertain whether she was going to mock him or not. 'You are in love with death and the past,' she said at last. And her voice left him uncertain still.

'Not exactly. It's just the quietness of death and the past, like the quietness after love.'

'Ah.' Her smile quickened at last. She had settled on mockery, then. 'You only make love to me in order to feel quiet afterwards?'

He shook his head lightly, laying his hand on her hair. 'But you do make me quiet. And that's why...'

'Why what?'

He watched his hand stroking the fine straight hair over her ear.

'Why what?'

'Would you stay with me for good if I asked you?'

'You mean marry you?'

'If that's not a dirty word,'

She smiled at him, holding his hand still on her head and stroking it thoughtfully.

'You've drawn curtains across your eyes, did you know that?'

'Have I?' The corners of her lips flickered into a smile, but her eyes were still veiled.

'Would you, if I asked you?'

'Would you ask me?'

'I'm thinking of it.'

Her lids drooped, the heavy Chinese lids that excited him as much as any other part of her body. 'But I do not think you ever will ask me...'

'Oh? 'Why?'

'You don't really want to leave Helen.'

'I really don't want to leave you.'

'But one day you will.' She was still lightly stroking the back of his hand.

'You think so?'

'People do leave me.'

"Why? Who?'

.'Perhaps ...' She shrugged off the second question. 'Perhaps they think I am too ... self-sufficient?'

'And are you?'

'I don't know.' She frowned. 'Besides, how would you tell Helen?'

'If I told her, would you live with me?'

'Your children would call me a dirty Chink.'

'Elena's very fond of you. Perhaps I'll tell her anyway.'

'Elena?'

'Helen, idiot.'

The curtains were drawn back from her eyes and they smiled at him, yet still gravely. 'So you would tell her without knowing whether I would live with you or not? And suppose afterwards I said I would not?'

'Things could hardly be worse than they are now.'

'And what about your children, where would they go? To their mother or to their father's mistress — or did you say second wife?'

He lay silent, thinking of Alexander and Elena, who were already inarticulately aware of the grating bitterness between Helen and himself.

'You would always feel guilty about it.' She was frowning again. 'And in any case, I don't know whether I could handle them.'

'You wouldn't like them?'

'They wouldn't like me… And you would always feel guilty about that … And then, there is my dancing,' she said, as if coming to a conclusion.

'How do you know I would feel guilty?'

'You feel guilty even now, as things are.'

'No —'

'And then you would be bitter and angry, like you are now about Helen. But it would be about me.'

He pulled her head closer, till his forehead touched hers. 'I'll keep on asking you till I wear you down.' He felt the wrinkles of her frown loosen against his forehead.

'I don't think I want you to stop *asking* me,' she said slowly.

He leant his head back to search her face for signs that she was teasing him again. 'Sometimes I think you're completely impenetrable.'

Now the mocking smile did appear in her eyes as they narrowed. 'Considering what you were doing to me half an hour ago,' she said precisely, 'I do not know why you should ever think that.'

Another corner of the cemetery contains the grave of the missionary and sinologue, Robert Morrison, whose career is summarised as follows: Sacred to the memory of Robert Morrison, D.D., the first Protestant Missionary to China, who after a service of twenty-seven years cheerfully spent in extending the Kingdom of the blessed Redeemer, during which period he compiled and published a dictionary of the Chinese language, founded the Anglo-Chinese College of Malacca and for several years laboured alone on a Chinese version of the Holy Scriptures, which he was spared to see completed and widely circulated amongst those for whom it was destined, he sweetly slept in Jesus. He was born at Morpeth in Northumberland January 5th 1782, was sent to China by the London Missionary Society in 1807, was for twenty-five years Chinese translator in the employ of the East India Company and died at Canton August 1st, 1834. Blessed are the dead which die in the Lord from henceforth, Yea, saith the Spirit, that they may rest from their labours and their works do follow them.

'What did he want?'

'It is a letter from my father.'

'Your father? How did it find its way here?'

She was turning the flimsy envelope over in her hands, frowning at the characters. 'I always leave my address, in case there is a letter from him.'

The afternoon sun was glaring harshly on to the balcony, but she went outside to read the letter by herself. Dimitri lay with his hands under his head, searching the cracked, stained plaster of the wall for the little tjik-tjak. But he did not look carefully, distracted by a vague apprehensiveness that Mila's letter had induced.

'I can't see our lizard friend any more,' he began, as she came back.

'Dimitri, I must go to Shanghai,' she said flatly. 'My father is sick. He says he is dying.'

She started packing at once, filling her case quietly and neatly.

'What's wrong with him, Mila?'

She didn't look up. 'He does not say.'

'I'd better pack too.' As he watched her, he began to feel she had gone already.

'You do not have to leave.'

'I don't want to stay, now that you're going.' He started rolling up the scroll on the door. He tied it up slowly and put it in the bottom of his bag. 'Will they let you out again, Mila?'

'They did before.' Her voice was tightening.

He stared into the emptiness of the bag. The scroll looked lost and forlorn in it. If it had been my father, would I have gone, as a matter of course? he asked himself. With all the risks? But I'm not Chinese. Aloud, he said slowly, 'It was easier before. Now, with all the troubles _'

'I have to go,' she cut him off. 'I am his daughter. It is not a stranger.'

'Well,' he sighed, 'in that case, I'd better go and see about the bill.'

> At the entrance to Macau's Inner Harbour stands the temple known as the Ma Kok Miu. The original shrine is said to have been erected by Fukienese fishing people early in the Ming dynasty or a little earlier and to have been sacred to the well-known sea goddess, Tin Hau. It is now known as the temple of the Fukienese sea Goddess Neung Ma, or of A-ma, whence the name of Macau (A-ma-kau).
>
> The Goddess is said to have been a maiden of Foochow who came to the waterfront to beg a free passage to Shanghai, but only the master of the poorest junk, who had few passengers, would consent to take her. On the way, a violent storm sank all the rich junks, while the maiden of Foochow took the tiller of her benefactor's vessel and brought it safely to Macau. No sooner had it reached land than she climbed a high rock and disappeared. The occupants of the boat knew therefore that they had been befriended by their patron deity and, as the story spread, contributions poured in for the erection of a temple to her.

TWO VANISH ACROSS THE BORDER
NEW SPATE OF BOMBINGS

Two men were taken across the border to China yesterday. One of them was apparently injured by a mine which he trod on while climbing a barbed wire fence at the Army position at Man Kam To. According to eye-witnesses, the man was seen to be injured and a doctor and ambulance were sent for. However, before they could arrive, two other men appeared on the scene and took him across the Shum Chun river into China. There was speculation last night about whether the injured man was intending to damage the military post at Man Kam To or to visit the graves of his ancestors. (It is known that the border position enclosed several family graves.)

In the other incident, a resident of Chuk Yuan village was attacked by four men as he was bicycling near Ta Ku Ling Police Station. After a fierce struggle, the man was dragged across the border before the police could come to his assistance. It was learned later that the man had been in a coffee shop at Ta Ku Ling earlier in the day, denouncing Chairman Mao and his book of 'Thoughts.' Fears were expressed for his safety last night.

In Hong Kong and Kowloon there was another rash of bomb incidents, in which a number of people were injured and one killed. Altogether there were fifty bomb reports and a large number of arrests. One bomb-thrower paid with his life when the bomb he was about to throw exploded prematurely. He was found near Wong Tau Hom Resettlement Estate, dying in a pool of blood with his right hand missing.

They stood together, Jan, Lisa and Dimitri, in a quiet semi-circle on the boat deck. Beneath and facing them, on the floodlit quay, stood the wider semi-circle of the Police Band. Half in darkness behind the band, a thin crowd waited for the boat to leave, waving, calling out and throwing paper streamers.

The bandmaster lifted the cuff of his white tropical tunic and glanced at his watch. A police siren was screaming distantly in Nathan Road. As he raised his baton, the crump of an exploding bomb sounded nearer by. The crowd laughed and cheered raggedly and Dimitri heard Jan snort. Undeterred, the bandmaster swung into 'Auld

Lang Syne' again, drowning the rising clamour of sirens. People in the crowd started singing and the passengers joined in, hoarse and out of tune. 'That must be the third time they play that song,' Jan muttered. 'Don't they know anything else?'

Dimitri smiled without answering. The gruffness in Jan's voice betrayed the emotion he was trying to hide. His heavy white hands were softly beating time on the wooden rail. Beside him, Lisa stood, painfully erect, clutching the bouquet of orchids awkwardly across her flat, narrow chest. The little card, in Chinese and English, was still clipped to one of the stems: *'Long life and happiness from The Hong Kong Police Benevolent Association'*.

Some muscle kept twitching in little spasms beneath the pale skin of her cheek. She too was moved, despite — or because — of the banal sentimentality of the occasion. She was gazing down at the band, now thumping through the closing bars, with a serious, abstracted expression. Dimitri was reminded of her words a few months ago — He's dreading it, it's like cutting his arm off — the only time she had ever unbent enough to touch him in all the years she had known him since childhood.

The last notes blared and faded and there was a moment's silence in the crowd. The bandsmen rested their instruments. The sirens were still wailing, further away now.

'It iss Wong Tai Sin again,' Jan said, cocking his head to listen. 'They should not have sent the band here, they ought to be on duty.'

Dimitri shrugged, looking down at the hazed halo of tropical humidity round the lamps on the quayside and at the crowds of night-insects swarming about them.

'But it iss not my job any more ...' Jan went on slowly. Then, after a long pause in which his fist kept lightly pounding the rail, 'It iss like a down-payment on death, retiring from your job...'

Lisa and Dimitri looked at him unsurely, then at each other. He's dreading it, Dimitri. It's like cutting his arm off.

Jan shrugged heavily and shook his head, as if he was throwing his thoughts off like a fly that had settled on his cheek. 'How much longer?' He avoided looking at Dimitri.

'It's five to twelve.'

The bandsmen had started chatting to each other. Voices called from the crowd too and streamers rustled through the air again. But the three of them could find nothing more to say. They stood looking down in heavy, brooding expectancy. It can't last much longer, Dimitri thought. If only it leaves on time.

'When iss the trial?' Jan glanced at Dimitri, for the first time.

'Next month.'

He grunted, seemed about to speak, then looked away again. Ever since he had warned Dimitri, he had kept off the subject of the trial. Dimitri's reaction had opened a little crevice between them which they stepped across warily, afraid it might widen.

The sirens had stopped. The bandsmen's words rose clearly to where they stood. One of them was asking complainingly how much longer before the ship sailed.

'Cantonese always sounds like recitative to me,' Dimitri tried to ease the tenseness of waiting. 'It's so incongruous too, Scottish music, Chinese faces.'

'Everything is incongruous in Hong Kong.' Lisa shrugged, disparaging either Hong Kong or her own trite remark.

Now, by tacit agreement, they gave up trying and let the silence possess them. They stood together but separately, each self-involved. And it had happened to the other passengers too, and the crowd. They were all waiting, giving up one after another their hollow jokes and cheeriness. They changed feet uneasily, checked their watches and searched the harbour for the tugboat.

At last a loud whoop announced it, and the tenseness eased. Dimitri, Lisa and Jan all looked at each other at the same moment, and smiled, with relief as much as sadness. The loudspeaker crackled over their heads.

'*Laos* va partir. *Laos* va partir. Tous les visiteurs sont priés de quitter le bateau.'

Dimitri held out his hand at once. 'Well...'

'Goodbye, Dimitri.'

'See you in England, next year I hope.'

'Yes. Good luck in your trial.'

He laughed, falsely. 'It's not my trial, Jan, it's theirs. I'm not accused of anything, you know...'

'Not *accused*, no,' Jan said abruptly.

'Goodbye, Lisa.' Her hand was cool and rigid. Only a flicker in her eyes gave her away.

The band was playing again as he went down the gangway. *Will ye no' come back again?*

Looking back from the crowd, Dimitri saw Jan and Lisa standing together in the shadows, grey-haired, stiff and still. They were looking not at him nor at the band, but far away across the city towards the Kowloon hills, or perhaps towards that distant town in Russia where Jan had lived his boyhood.

The deep, throbbing blast of the liner's siren echoed round the harbour, answered by three short whoops from the tug. *Laos* moved with a massive calmness slowly away. As the dark, oily water gradually widened between the ship and the quay, the band stopped playing. With an indifference to the poignant which no longer disconcerted Dimitri, they trudged away just when the parting should have been at its climax. Streamers were snapping, hands waving, raucous voices bellowing last messages across the growing separation, but the bandsmen had done their stint and were on their way home.

Dimitri waved. Jan lifted his hand and let it fall heavily, as if he too could not sustain the ceremony of leave-taking any longer.

The long white liner dismissed the tug with another reverberating blast of its siren and turned slowly broadside on. The lights of Victoria glittered like a million steady candles in the dark behind her. For a moment she lay still, then the white wake began to churn at her stern and she moved away towards the Lyemun Pass. Jan was scarcely distinguishable now, a blurred grey shape beside a smaller shape under a lifeboat davit. The ship slipped inexorably away, a cross-harbour ferry took her momentarily from view, released her again, and then she had merged into the dark.

Dimitri realised that all the crowd had gone by now and he was standing alone.

He walked slowly out of the terminal. It was a quarter past midnight, but the street was still crowded. People had got used to the bomb-throwing which had replaced the demonstrations and riots of a few months ago. An explosion, some shots, some blood, a gathering crowd of silent onlookers, the sirens of police trucks and ambulances, and then everyone went on as before. The fear that China might take over Hong Kong had gradually receded into the unvisited backs of people's minds and the daily bomb report was becoming accepted like the weather forecast, a part of normal life. We could even get used to the idea that the world was going to end next week, he thought as he watched the neon-lights winking and glaring in all their extravagant vulgarity and the buses, taxis and rickshaws streaming incessantly past. We would simply behave as though it could not be — our strength and our weakness.

He strolled towards Nathan Road. The bar where Julie worked was in one of the little side streets creeping furtively away from it. It was not until he had started walking that he realised that he was going there.

He was passing the site on Hankow Road where his mother's store had stood, long since demolished. And the memories which Jan's departure had brought crowding to the threshold of his mind now came tumbling through.

When the war ended and he boarded the grey British warship with his mother, both emaciated, hardly able to walk, Jan had pushed a battered tin of smuggled corned beef into his hands. And Dimitri had cried as the ship sailed, as if Jan had been his father.

The drawing-room in North London, barely warmed by the few smouldering, smoking coals in the grate. His white-haired English grandparents, one each side of the hearth, rubbing their raw, cold hands together and complaining, about someone called Attlee... His mother sitting on the bed while he was half-asleep, whispering to him in the Russian his grandparents said he ought not to speak... The undercurrent of hostility between his mother and his grandparents, of which he obscurely realised he was partly the cause, erupting at last in an open quarrel in the chill of the unheated dining-room... His grandparents icy and sharp, his mother crying and incoherent.

'Dimitri I'm going back to Hong Kong.' she had said to him later in the bedroom.

'What about me?

'You'll come in the holidays. You have to go to school.'

'Will Jan be there?

The long blank years of his minor public school, faceless and unrememberable now, their backs turned towards him. Except that it was then that the nightmares of the Japanese soldier began to haunt him, the soldier who had shot the Chinese policeman on the Peak in Hong Kong, as casually as shooting a rabbit. Strange that his father's lingering, ugly death from dysentery, which he had watched in solemn, anxious silence from the corner of his prison hut, had bred no similar monster in the darker spaces of his mind. But there was another nightmare that also came then, that of the slick thud of bamboo clubs on bone and bleeding flesh.

His grandparents took him out to tea once a month during terms, in a mock-Tudor tea shop that smelled of cats and always seemed to be empty. During the Easter and Christmas holidays, he stayed with them, oppressed by an atmosphere of genteel gloom and damp decay. But every summer he flew back to Hong Kong, where his mother's shop made just enough money to pay his fares.

Jan had rejoined the police, For a time he was in the marine division and sometimes he took Dimitri with him on police launches to the outlying islands that lay like grey, sun-baked stepping stones in the waveless, glittering sea. The little fishing villages that straggled along their shores, and the farmhouses amongst the pools of light green paddy fields, seemed to he the only things in Hong Kong that had not changed since then. Here, where he was walking, almost nothing stood now that had stood twenty years ago. He could not even place the exact spot where his mother's shop had been. But in those villages he could still walk the same paths between the same fields and see the same life. Yet even they were near their death. One more generation, and the children would all become factory workers in the new towns, the fields overgrown, the fishing junks beached, the houses broken, empty shells.

Were Jan and Lisa still gazing at the last lights of these islands, the lights of what had, substantially, been their life? Or had they already dipped below the horizon, the final amputation of their working lives?

He's dreading it Dimitri. It's like cutting his arm off.

His mother's shop. It used to sell year-old styles to rich Chinese ladies with rings on every finger and to not so rich colonial servants' wives with sun-shrivelled faces and loud, overbearing voices. Jan and Lisa used to come often to the little flat over the shop, where his mother, as Jan put it, 'held court' in the evenings. Russians, Poles, Jews, filtered into Hong Kong through the sieves of Harbin, Japan, Shanghai, even Tibet, would gather beneath the soothingly-whirring fans to drink coffee or tea — there was even a samovar at first — while they smoked, gossiped, played ancient, scratchy records and hatched dubious business deals. Reuben Sternor, brilliantined hair, sad yet shrewd brown eyes, was always there, and Jan, ebullient and loud, with

Lisa, quiet and severe. His mother's blonde hair had turned drab and lustreless and her face had become lined with the strains of business cares, but she always changed her dress and put on make-up for these evenings, which revived, although in worn and wistful forms, the lost society of her Petersburg childhood.

His grandparents died within six months of each other in the year before he went up to Cambridge. He spent most of that year in Hong Kong relearning Cantonese and discovering for the first time the lonely tedium of his mother's life. She lost business to smarter competitors and the number of her court dwindled from year to year with death and onward migration. Her health began to fray and she seldom left the shop then except for unavailing visits to the doctor. Dimitri drove all over the colony on a secondhand motor scooter and visited every little village, coming home late at night to the bitter and fearful remonstrances of his deserted, ailing mother.

'He comes home so late because he has a girl in Wanchai, Jan told her cheerily. 'What do you think? He iss a monk?'

But in fact he had been so cloistered by his grandparents and mildly homosexual school upbringing that he was morbidly shy of girls.

At last, primed with drink, quaking with uncertainties, he crooked his finger at a pretty bar-girl. She laughed at him good-temperedly and took him to her sleazy room above a side-street fruit shop. He could still recall the tall pyramids of large mandarin oranges inside it. She had bought two of them before she led him up the narrow, dingy stairs, while the shop-owner, in shorts and singlet, mockingly congratulated her on capturing a virgin. When he left a couple of hours later, the shop was shut and barred but the owner was squatting on the dirty sidewalk outside, smoking a cigarette that might have been heroin. He glanced up at Dimitri indifferently now and spat into the gutter.

Dimitri was slow to develop sensuality. He had not slept with another woman until he met Helen in Cambridge two years later. And he never experienced the full pleasure of a woman, the pleasure which was neither inhibited nor forced, until Helen's chilling repulses, the sombreness of their marriage, and, the, slow erosion of his intellectual hopes and ambitions had gathered all together into a blind, thrusting towards sensuous self-forgetfulness.

The blast of a ship's siren again, shuddering round the harbour, brought him back to Jan. Now that Jan and Lisa had gone, was it only Reuben Sternor who was left to remind him of his childhood? Almost nobody and nothing else. So now middle age confronts you, he thought, with a trite gloomy rhetoric that satisfied him even while he smiled in ridicule at it. And behind it stands old age and behind that death.

He went down the dimly lit steps into the Sole Bar.

A swarthy Filipino Combo was strumming listlessly to an almost deserted room. At a table in the corner, a few bar-girls were playing cards, bored and twittering. The bulky mamasan was negotiating with a middle-aged European in unsubdued whispers the price he would have to pay to buy a girl out for the rest of the night. The girl, a tall, disdainful Shanghainese, sealed the bargain by getting the man to buy the mamasan a drink. After perfunctory thanks and a fractional smile, she agreed to a fee of sixty-five dollars and the girl led her customer away like a blushing, docile child, while she sang out brassy goodbyes to the girls at the table.

The mamasan smiled at Dimitri — he was well known there — but he did not invite her to have a drink. He sat at the bar alone, gazing down at the saucer of peanuts the barman had placed beside his beer, while ragged, fleeting thoughts of Helen, Mila and Jan slipped across the dulled surface of his mind. But as the Filipinos droned into another sugary tune, a black American draped himself, rather than sat, on the stool beside him.

'Hi, man, what ship you on?'

'No ship. I live here.'

'You live here? Jesus Christ, let's rap, man.' He swung round on his stool and leaned towards Dimitri. He was wearing knee-length black boots, blue jeans, a purple silk shirt and a peaked blue cap on the back of his head. The loose, swinging grace of the Black was slurred in him, from either drink or drugs. His arm swept along the counter, knocking the peanuts onto the floor, but he did not notice. 'Fix me a special,' he said carelessly to the barman, with a trace of the easy arrogance that perhaps he might have experienced from a white man in Mississippi.

'What kind special drink?'

'Hell, I don't care, man. The best you got.'

'You want whisky?'

Yeah, whisky-'

'Whisky sour you want?'

'Hey, leave me alone, will ya? I want to rap with this fella here. Yeah, whisky sour.'

Dimitri turned to him resignedly. 'What ship are you on?'

'Supply ship.' He had a long drooping moustache and he kept smiling with dazed good humour.

'From Vietnam?'

'Veetnahm, right. Hey, you a stoker, man?'

'No, I live here.'

'Where d'you come from? You British?'

'I'm afraid so.'

'Shit, you're the first Britisher I ever spoke to.' He clapped a friendly hand on Dimitri's shoulder. 'The first goddamn Britisher I ever spoke to ... What ship you on, man? Hell, them dude British tin-cans, I see them in Manila ... Into port, dressed whites. Outa port dressed whites. That's a navy, man. Shit, the U.S. Navy's gone to shit, man. All fucked up. Ya know them British tin-cans ... What d'you call 'em? Destroyers? You got names or numbers? Man, I tell you that's a real navy. Dressed in whites into port, dressed in whites outa port. We just looked like stokers, man. U.S. Navy's all gone to shit.'

Dimitri felt a light tap on his shoulder, which he knew was Julie. She slipped on to the stool the other side of him, leaned across as if to kiss his cheek, then bit his ear instead.

'Hey, this your chick, man?'

'Sort of.' He smiled at Julie with relief, glad of an excuse to turn away from the sailor. He spoke to her in Cantonese, nodding to the hovering barman to pour her a drink. 'How are things?'

'Fine.' She shrugged and pouted, answering in English. She watched the barman pour her a thimbleful of what looked like rum, but Dimitri and she both knew was cold tea. 'Long time no see.' She would never speak Cantonese with him in the bar. Her tiny pidgin vocabulary gave her status over the other girls who could not speak even that much English. To have spoken Cantonese with Dimitri in front of them would have been to imply that he found her English unintelligible — an unacceptable loss of face. When they were alone, though, she always spoke Cantonese. It was more than just a switch of languages — her personality changed too, from the conventional, sulky, would-be sophisticated bar-girl to the naive, vivacious fisherman's daughter.

'Where you been?' She was still eyeing him under sulkily drooping lids. 'You find other one girl-friend?'

'Yes.' He looked at her frankly. 'She's in China now.'

'Huh.' She raised her brows disbelievingly, lifting her glass with that casual, finger-crooking delicacy that no European, not even a princess, would ever match.

'Like we got a radio operator.' The American left his stool to stand unsteadily between them. 'That guy can take signals from any godamm ship in the world. And you know where the bureau assigned him? He's been assigned to paint the fuckin' ship. Why, he could take signals from any fuckin' ship in the U.S. Navy, man, and they tell him to paint it. That's the U.S. Navy. Gone to shit. This your girl?'

'Sort of.'

Julie looked him up and down with insulting disdain. To her, dark skins were dirty and smelly. Very few bar-girls would go with a Black or an Indian.

'What've you been doing? Dimitri asked her.

'Same same.'

'Say, what're all these bombs in Hong Kong? It's like Saigon, man. You guys protecting Hong Kong? You fightin' the gooks off ?,

'Not exactly.'

'Well, that sure is a damn fine navy, man. Better than the fuckin' U.S. Navy. Ain't a man on board doesn't want to quit. Gone to shit, the U.S. Navy.'

'How's business, Julie?'

'Same same. You been busy?'

'No, I've got to go to court, though.'

'Court?'

He went on in Cantonese. 'Someone was killed in the riots. While he was in prison. I saw the police beating him up. So there's going to be a trial.'

She shrugged again, indifferently. 'When?'

'Next month.'

'No can hurt police.'

'Them British tin-cans were all dressed in white at Manila, man, and we just looked like fuckin' stokers.'

'What you waste time for?'

'What ship you on? You an engineer? Oiler?'

The flower woman appeared in the doorway and made towards them. She had a shuffle that suggested her feet must have been bound once and her ageing face had a bruised, gentle expression. Twenty years ago she had been a bar-girl. Now she supported her son in an American college by selling stolen roses round the bars.

'Buy me a flower.'

'All gone to shit, man, the U.S. Navy. Soviets are number one naval power now, man. The Soviets 've got better ships and better crews. Shit, the U.S. Navy...'

He bought Julie a wilting pink rose. She laid it on the bar beside her glass.

'... Shit-scared to fire them ol' missiles in case they come right back down the stack and blow 'em up...'

'Hey, sailor,' Julie laid her dainty hand on his thick brown wrist. 'You need anything?'

'What you got to give me?'

'You want buy some powder?'

He became suddenly alert. 'What's the price?'

'Julie, what are you up to now?' Dimitri took her hand off the sailor's, speaking in Cantonese.

'You want to tell my fortune?' she answered in Cantonese too, turning her palm upwards in his. 'Want to tell my fortune?'

'What are you mixed up in now?'

'Make money. You want to tell my fortune?' She looked up at him sullenly, returning to English. 'Beside, you not care, you got other one girl-friend.' Her eyes seemed suddenly to be glistening over-brightly, the pupils unnaturally wide. 'You mind own business, uh?'

'You stupid bitch,' he said slowly.

She pulled her hand away, turning back to the American. 'How much you need? Maybe I can get.'

CONFIDENTIAL

Mr Johnston has some very good qualifications for this post. He is said to be an excellent teacher and his research, with which we are familiar, is certainly of a high quality. Unfortunately, though, it is not very considerable as regards quantity. The committee feels some reservation on this score; candidates for a post of this seniority would ordinarily be expected to have published rather more than Mr Johnston. He has not perhaps been sufficiently stimulated in the intellectual environment of Hong Kong to press ahead rapidly with his research and produce more work of the merit he is obviously capable of. Can we expect him to fulfil his earlier promise at the age which he has now reached? The committee is unable to convince itself that he will. It is known that he is working on a book, which may substantially enhance his reputation as a scholar. But progress, as he himself acknowledges, has been slow. Without definite information on which to form an estimate of this piece of research, the committee feels unable to recommend Mr Johnston's appointment.

Of the other two candidates assessed ...

Peter Frankam H.K. Club 1 p.m. Lunch.

Dimitri got out of the taxi at Statue Square. The tall fountains rose still and glistening in the breathless sunlight, unnoticed by the swift-stepping crowds crossing and recrossing the square in dedicated pursuit of the fast buck. Neatly dressed typists, clerks or businessmen, all were hurrying to hatch deals or place bets over lunch or coffee, a thousand dollars or twenty-five, each bargaining relentlessly to the last profitable cent. Yesterday, several bombs had been planted here. One man was shot and thirty-seven people injured by shrapnel. Today, there were still a few dark, ignored stains on the sun-glaring white paving stones. Tomorrow even they would be gone, scuffed out by a million scurrying feet.

Overlooking all this restless activity stood the ugly concrete masses of the Hong Kong and Shanghai Bank, the Chartered Bank and Prince's Shopping Arcade. Somehow, through their bare, characterless windows, they seemed to emanate a bleak air of proprietary approval at the manifest triumph of capitalism before their doors. Directly opposite were the Supreme Court and the Hong Kong Club, revealing, in their nineteenth-century architecture, a certain restraint the twentieth century lacked. A little to the east, the Bank of China rose, narrower, but even higher than the others, its top spiky with iron bars to prevent police helicopters from landing. The Bank of China was the unofficial Chinese embassy and, although it had directed many of the riots and demonstrations, neither the police nor the army had ever entered it, tacitly admitting its diplomatic immunity. Its windows were smaller and more forbidding than the other banks' and, whatever expression they wore, Dimitri smiled wrily, it certainly wasn't approving.

He walked slowly across the square, letting the crowd scurry ant-like round him. He could just hear the hissing spray of the fountains above the noise of the traffic and it occurred to him that none of the people dodging past him were talking. Each one was a separate parcel of energy and aims, without any interest in the others, except as possible rivals.

The club was the oldest building still standing in the city centre, colonnaded and shuttered on three storeys. Dimitri was not a member and the doorman eyed him unsurely until he asked for Mr Frankam. Peter was giving the lunch in an upstairs room. Waiting for the lift, Dimitri glanced round the lobby. The walls were painted a fading lime green. A number of rubber plants stood along them, their leaves shiny as if they had been polished. The notice board beside him caught his eye.

In accordance with article 329 (Payment of Monies) the undernoted members' names are hereby noted in the main hall for non-payment of dues:

The lift doors slid open and he stepped in. The faint mustiness, the green of the walls and the tone of the notice recalled smudged memories of his school in England. It was as though this place too were damp, cold and gloomy, despite the summer's heat — a rheumatism of the heart. He walked down the long, worn, red carpet of the hall, silent and empty as a cathedral, and paused at the doorway. He felt as vaguely apprehensive as he used to feel when called to the headmaster's study at school. Glasses were chinking with ice, voices were chatting smoothly, and suddenly he wanted to run away before Peter saw him. There slipped into his mind a memory of the school photograph his mother used to keep on her bedroom wall. He could see his face in the second row left, head down, withdrawn eyes shyly, almost sullenly, peering up at the camera, arms stiffly folded across his chest, the cuffs of his grey school jacket much too short.

'Dimitri, how are you?' Peter came to meet him. He was as sleek as ever, fair hair too beautifully in place and tie, a delicate purple, too carefully chosen for effect against the pale blue shirt and trim grey suit.

'Glad you could come. We haven't met for months, it seems. How is Helen?'

Three equally well-dressed, but more imposing-looking men were standing together in the room, drinks in their hands. They turned to Dimitri, glowing corporately, it seemed, with the warmth of self-satisfaction.

'I expect you know everyone?' Peter began, with only the faintest trace of doubt in his slightly unctuous voice.

'The exact contrary, I'm afraid.'

'Oh.' A little discomposed by his abruptness, Peter introduced him quickly to a judge with a deep sun tan and slightly pendulous jowl, a Chinese manufacturing taipan who bowed and smiled with reserved politeness and a colonel in the Gurkha Brigade, wearing a Christ Church tie, who had just arrived in Hong Kong. Dimitri remembered their names from the announcements in the *Morning Post*, where anyone with money and every government official who came or left was solemnly commemorated.

He felt the three pairs of eyes estimating him while Peter ordered a drink from the white-jacketed waiter. 'I have the advantage of you all,' he began with an awkward dryness, 'I know all about you from the newspapers, whereas you can't possibly know anything about me, since I'm never in them.'

'Oh, Peter's been telling us what a brilliant chap you are and all that,' drawled the colonel in unmistakably Christ Church tones. 'And I dare say he's more reliable than your average newspaper…' There was a suggestion of irony in his voice, strengthened by the narrowing of his rather close-set brown eyes, which hinted that his casual manner was merely a carefully preserved facade behind which some fairly deft mental operations were being conducted.

'His information is more accurate, I'm sure, but his editorial comments may be equally… '

'Perverse?' suggested Peter, smiling faultlessly at himself as he handed Dimitri his glass. 'I was just telling them about this trial you're involved in.'

'Fortunately I won't be trying it,' interrupted the judge. His pendulous jowls gave him a mournful look which his phlegmy, sepulchral voice did nothing to alleviate. 'Otherwise one of us would have to leave.'

'When are you stepping into the box?' the colonel asked.

'Couple of weeks now.' He turned to Peter, who was fingering his tie. 'Have there been any murmurs of dissatisfaction about it? About prosecuting two policemen, I mean, at a time when they're all getting picked off by the opposition?'

'No doubt there was some heart-searching before the decision to prosecute was taken.' Peter pursed his lips consideringly. 'The morale of the force was very important just then — still is, of course. They're still the main target for bombs and knives and so on ... I would imagine the average bobby here feels rather aggrieved that his colleagues should be tried for getting their own back in what is a time-honoured way, after all ...'

'Yes, we had the same problem in Cyprus.' The colonel stretched and threw back his shoulders, reminding Dimitri momentarily of Jan. 'Terrorism always provokes some kind of counter-terrorism. And that's how revolutions get their martyrs, I suppose ... You never get a decent revolution without a bunch of martyrs, after all. Absolute *sine qua non*. Absolute.'

'Well, I hope these aggrieved coppers won't try to tamper with the witnesses ...' Dimitri was wondering how far he could probe.

'Have you been tampered with?' asked the taipan.

'I'm probably not so vulnerable as... others might be.'

'Oh, I think that sort of thing always comes to light, you know,' the judge wheezed a little. 'After all, we do have a rule of law here.. .'

Dimitri shrugged, thinking of Mila, and of Jan's warning.

The others resumed the conversation his entrance had interrupted, profitable investments in the Hong Kong stock market. Dimitri sipped his drink, half-listening. The taipan spoke in thick fluent English about the speculative nature of the market and the possibility of making vast profits just then because the communist disturbances had pushed share prices down to an unreal level.

'But if the disturbances grow worse?' asked the judge.

'Yes, yes. It is all speculative,' the taipan opened his hands and laughed. 'If your horse dies before the finishing post, you lose your money. It happened in Shanghai.'

The colonel began to reveal the alertness Dimitri had suspected, comparing quotations on the Hong Kong and London exchanges with the taipan. Peter tried to bring the judge and Dimitri into this discussion, but neither responded. The judge turned to Dimitri behind the taipan's back, eyeing him thoughtfully.

'You don't sail a boat by any chance, do you? At the yacht club?'

'No, I'm afraid not.'

'Ah. Thought I might have seen you there.' He looked down at his glass resignedly. 'Well, I always was bad on faces...'

The soup was placed on a table beside the lace-curtained window. Dimitri sat between the colonel and the taipan, who had to adjourn their financial discussion. The colonel had no difficulty in changing topics, though.

'And what are all the brilliant minds thinking at the university these days?'

'Many of them are as keenly interested in the stock market as you are,' Peter returned the irony. 'Although that doesn't always indicate a brilliant mind, of course.'

'Dimitri is too modest to mention that he's writing a book.' Peter bent towards him from the head of the table.

'No doubt it will be brilliant,' murmured the colonel.

'How is it going, Dimitri?'

'Backwards at present.'

'Oh, I'm sure that's more modesty — false modesty. I've told everyone already that you're the only person in Hong Kong who's equally at home in Russian and Chinese literature.'

He couldn't let me be a mediocrity, Dimitri thought as he crumbled some bread on the tablecloth. It would never do to admit be knew anyone undistinguished.

'And what do you think of Confucius, Mr Johnston?' the taipan asked, dabbing at some soup on his hairless chin. 'Can he be translated?'

'Only by a schizophrenic.' He supposed that was why each of them had been invited, to impress the others and glorify His Nibs.

He talked stiltedly with the taipan, who was careful to let him know he had his suits made in Savile Row, about Shanghai before the communist take-over. It was better than Hong Kong, the taipan said, because the profits were even higher.

'The workers knew it was work or starve. So they worked.' And his keen eyes sparkled as he laughed.

On Dimitri's other side, the colonel was maintaining the Gurkhas were such good fighters because they had no imagination and so no fear.

'Still, don't you think they'd fight in vain if they had to defend Hong Kong against the PLA?' Peter asked.

'Oh, I suppose we could fight a holding action until the necessary notables had been evacuated ...' He scratched his bristly grey moustache. 'Not that I think it's a probability any more, you know ... There were some tricky months, of course, but I can't see Peking doing anything now, since it didn't move when things were more critical. After all,' he raised his eyes quizzically towards the taipan, 'wouldn't you say John Chinaman knows a good bargain when he sees one? Whether he's a Maoist or a mandarin? And Hong Kong's likely to be a good bargain for China for some time yet, with all the foreign exchange and information she gets through here. Barring unforeseen accidents, I should say the worst is over ...'

The next course came and Dimitri withdrew more and more from the conversation, unable either to follow or break the conventions of sophisticated chatter in which the others, except the melancholic judge, excelled. He gazed out of the window at the heat-hazed hills of Kowloon, beyond which the colonel's unimaginative Gurkhas were preparing patiently for the battle he thought would never come. And remote beyond them was Mila. Gone now for three weeks and no idea when she's coming back. Or if. She may even miss the trial. His eyes, following his thoughts, started searching amongst the crowded buildings of Kowloon city for the block where her now empty flat was. Though unsuccessful — you couldn't see Nathan Road from there — his search composed an image of her in his mind, built up of fluctuating memories of her gestures and expressions. If she does come back and tells her story at the trial, he thought, she might get her visa and go to England. Whereas now that I've missed that job, I'll just stay here and rot. Yes, I shall rot here.

The colonel's voice recalled him to the public world. 'You've been here a long time — born here, so Peter tells me... What's the view like from the seat of learning in your ivory tower? How d'you find the place?'

'It's a good place to rot in.'

'Oh come, that's a bit severe.' He laughed. '*I* don't mean to rot here.'

'Nobody *means* to.'

'Can't say I share your rather depressing *Weltanschauung,* all the same.' He laughed again, glancing round at the others for support.

'I wouldn't say that writing a book was rotting exactly,' Peter bridged the gap of silence. 'I mean composition is hardly a form of decomposition, would you say?'

'P'raps he means his book is rotten, what?' the colonel asked genially. 'More false modesty, no doubt.'

Dimitri shrugged, smiling helplessly down at his glass, as much ashamed of his absurd rhetoric as annoyed by their imperturbable complacence. And he didn't even mean what he'd said, he thought guiltily. He liked the place, he was in his own way a native.

The taipan saved him from further baiting by asking Peter whether it was true that he was going to become head of his department in the government.

Peter glanced down with a modesty that must have been studied. 'As a matter of fact you've hit the nail on the head.'

'Ah.'

'It's not official yet, of course, so don't breathe a word, will you?'

'Good show,' muttered the colonel, while the judge murmured some indistinct sounds of congratulation.

The taipan raised his glass gaily. "To our next Director.'

The others drank with slightly forced enthusiasm, while Peter smiled and shrugged deprecatingly. Watching him over his uplifted glass, Dimitri realised that this was why the lunch had been arranged, so that Peter could let his promotion be known and admired. Ever since he had first met Dimitri at Cambridge, Peter had been trying to impress him. Failing to get a first-class degree had only intensified his determination to extract at last the tribute that Dimitri had always a little contemptuously withheld. Peter's glance, meeting his and then dropping again, seemed to confirm his intuition. Now that he was to be Director of his department he could clearly be seen, in his own eyes at least, to have got ahead of Dimitri. But Peter wanted *him* to see it too, to have to admit it. Dimitri finished his wine musingly. Which of us is worse off, he wondered — he with his pathetic craving for praise or me with my inability to do anything that deserves it?

He left as soon as the coffee had been served. Peter walked with him to the door, lighting a cigar as he talked. His face was flushed with well-being and wine, but his eyes flickered inquiringly at Dimitri, still seeking the acknowledgement of his due. As Dimitri stolidly withheld it, though, Peter prompted him.

'You won't take it any further, Dimitri, will you? My elevation to the demigods, I mean. It won't be official for a month ...'

'No, of course not.' He still held back maliciously from congratulating him. 'I won't even tell Helen.'

'Ah,' he recovered quickly, 'and how is she, by the way? When is she coming back?'

'According to her last letter, as late as possible.'

'She doesn't want to?'

'Not particularly. She's never really liked the place. And then...' He felt he was giving away too much, but he let it go now. 'And then there is the *ennui* of matrimony too...'

'Mm.' Peter glanced at him sideways. 'And perhaps some of your... extramural activities have come to her notice as well?'

'Extramural?'

'A certain dancer?' He smiled and winked. 'A lady sometimes seen on television.'

Dimitri felt his face flushing.

'Mum's the word, eh?' He was leering roguishly now. 'I'll keep quiet about you and you'll keep quiet about me, eh?' He drew on his cigar and let the blue smoke waft up between them, smiling at Dimitri all the time with slightly bloodshot eyes.

'It's most considerate of you to show such tender regard for other people's wives.' He realised that Peter must be very drunk. 'I'm sure you'll make an excellent Director, with so much information at your disposal. Provided you always hold your liquor like a gentleman, of course.'

'Oh, but I always do.'

Dimitri walked slowly away down the long, red-carpeted hall. Someone was waiting by the lift, so he went down by the stairway. He let his hand brush the stone balustrade, thinking of Peter's leering face. If Peter knew about Mila, other people must know too. Sooner or later it would get to Helen, but he felt his will was paralysed, unable to choose either sooner or later. Perhaps it would all be over by then, anyway. Peter's gloating assumption that Mila could only be a *fille de joie*, a stealthy pleasure taken while Helen's back was turned, almost amused him, but there was another thought that nagged. Does he know more than he said? Does he have any idea she's been got at about the trial? If so, the getting at her must be an official plan. In which case, the whole thing's been cooked beforehand.

He walked out past the silent rubber trees into the bustling square. It was late October, but the sun was still fierce. A beggar was squatting in the shade of the Supreme Court, holding out a red plastic beaker for alms.

But surely an official conspiracy would have prevented a prosecution altogether?

Nobody gave the beggar any money, but he held his beaker up all the same.

Well, perhaps we'll know in a couple of weeks, one way or the other, Dimitri thought. I'll hold up my bit of evidence like he holds up his mug.

Haven't been to a single concert. My mother is getting past baby-sitting and the children hate being left alone in a strange place. I met Ian Smither on Regent Street. He is principal clarinet now. He was full of himself and so self-satisfied. I never liked his playing anyway. He asked me what I was doing and I said nothing, bringing up children. He was on his way to a rehearsal. At first I felt bitter but then I thought I wouldn't want to do it any more, so what does it matter. It's all been driven out of me by now.

Mother is much frailer than last time. She keeps forgetting things and the children make fun of her. They are so restless and their squabbling never stops. Elena misses you and keeps on asking why you can't come and leave your book for a while. Alex doesn't ask so much, but the other night he said people should only have holidays separately if they were divorced.

I've got reservations on the BOAC flight on November 15th. It goes straight through. I can't face stopping and sight-seeing any more and the children aren't interested. I feel sort of panic-stricken at the thought of coming back and dropping into that horrible, never-ending routine again. If I could think of a way out I'd take it, but there isn't any. Don't meet us at the airport. We haven't got much baggage and we can take a taxi.

Sorry this isn't a happy letter. I can't write happy letters any more, perhaps I never could.

Dimitri sat chewing his thumbnail while he reread the page he had just written. He frowned. Locked up in the prison of stale, flat sentences were a few fresh ideas, but they needed to be set free. He winced as his teeth tore a piece of nail away from the flesh, leaving an ugly, raw scar behind.

The phone buzzed on his desk. 'Yes?'

'May I speak to Mr Johnston, please?'

'Mila!'

'Dimitri.' Her voice was as calm and low as ever.

'When did you get back?'

'About half an hour ago.'

'They let you through all right? Both ways?'

'Otherwise I would not be here.' The separated syllables mocked him gently.

He waited for her to go on, but she said nothing.

'You always do that, you know?'

'What?'

'Wait for the other person to speak first.'

'Yes, you have told me before.'

Still she waited. At last he gave way. 'What happened in Shanghai?'

'My father died.'

'Oh. I'm sorry.'

'And what happened in Hong Kong?' she asked composedly.

'Nothing much. Bombs and so on... Oh yes, I didn't get that job. The one in London.'

She didn't answer. The line seemed to have died.

'Mila? Mila?'

'Yes, I was thinking about it.' She seemed to dismiss it now. 'And Helen?'

'Not back yet. Not till after the trial. You nearly missed it, you know.'

'Yes. There are all sorts of summonses and things inside the door.'

He could picture her suddenly in the flat, the windows still shut, the air stale and hot. 'Shall I come over, Mila?'

'I think perhaps later. I have to think about things. I am not ...'

'Harmonious?'

'Yes. I am not harmonious yet. And I have to think about the trial.'

'Why? That's another two days.'

'But I think it is better after the trial. I shall not feel free until then. I would like us to meet after the trial.'

'All right.'

'What are you doing now, Dimitri?'

He looked down at his torn thumbnail. It was beginning to bleed.

'Dimitri?'

'Yes, I was thinking about it.'

'Are you angry?'

'Just paying you back.'

'I am sorry.'

'Mila, has anything new happened? About the trial?'

'No, but I want to think about it, so I will not feel free with you now. Would not,' She corrected herself. 'I would not feel free.'

'What will you think about the trial?'

'Not just the trial. Everything.'

MORE TERROR BOMBS GREET LORD SHEPHERD

As predicted in the *Wen Wei Po* and other communist papers, there has been a great increase in bomb planting since Lord Shepherd, Minister of State for Commonwealth Affairs, arrived in the Colony for consultation with the governor. In the past three days there have been nearly five hundred bomb reports, five people have died and more than fifty been injured, many seriously. Police have made many arrests, the most significant being the capture of a high-ranking member of the 'All Circles Anti-Persecution Struggle Committee', who has been wanted by the police for several months.

A bomb took the life of a police constable near Tonnochy Road, when a suspicious object be was guarding whilst waiting for a demolition expert suddenly exploded. Two other policemen and a number of spectators were also injured. An eighteen-year-old youth died in hospital of injuries sustained when a bomb was thrown on to a crowded tram in Hennessy Road. The terrorists themselves suffered casualties when three men blew themselves up outside Ngau Tau Kok low-cost housing estate in Kowloon. One was found by police stretched out in a gutter, his right forearm, the right half of his face, his right eye and his teeth all missing. He was dead on arrival at the hospital. The second was also encountered in the gutter; he had multiple injuries, part of his jaw was missing and both his hands had been blown away. He died in hospital early the following morning. The third was eventually caught by police in a store in Wong Tai Sin. He was bereft of both his hands and had other severe injuries. He has been charged and is being kept in the custodial ward.

It is understood that Lord Shepherd is discussing the security situation in the Colony and will report back to the cabinet on his return to London.

Picture (left) shows the mutilated bomb-planter being taken away in agony by police and ambulance men. (Right) Relatives consoling the grief-stricken family of the police constable killed near Tonnochy Road.

Ah Wong followed him as he wheeled the two bicycles down the hall. He propped the boy's one up on its stand in Alex's room at the foot of his bed.

'How do you like them?' he asked her in Cantonese.

She shook her head so that her long plaited queue trembled down the back of her white tunic. 'Very dirty. Nowhere to keep them.'

'They won't stay in the bedrooms. They can leave them in the hall outside the door.' He wheeled the girl's bike into Elena's room. There were no bedclothes on the mattresses. It made the rooms look cold and bare.

'How much did they cost?' Ah Wong was bending down to look at the trade-mark, a little bronzed plaque on the glossy red paint.

'Not much. Two hundred and thirty dollars each. They're Japanese.'

She straightened up, sighing. 'Japanese things are no good.' People from her village had been shot by the Japanese and she hated them implacably. Dimitri had not dared to bring home a Japanese student once, for fear she would insult him. 'Why didn't you buy British ones?'

'Too expensive.' He played on her parsimony. He had wanted to buy the even cheaper Chinese ones which were sold by the local communist stores. But the shop he tried had just been raided by the police, who had poured tar over the windows to cover the anti-British slogans. The girl assistants, who knew him well and used to chat with him, refused to speak now. And a man in blue dungarees with a large Mao badge in his lapel asked him to leave, with gestures that were half-embarrassed and half-menacing.

'Very dirty,' Ah Wong said again, patting the uncovered pillow on Elena's bed discontentedly.

'They must play.'

'When are the children coming back?'

'Next week.'

She sniffed. 'Is missy coming back too?'

He glanced at her sharply. 'Yes of course.' She had never liked Helen, resenting her anxious interference in the kitchen and washroom. Helen could never leave her alone, not because she wanted to boss her, but because she felt she ought to. There was continuous warfare between them, polite, contemptuous disobedience from Ah Wong and fretful, unavailing hints, nervous reproofs, from Helen.

He went to look out of the window. It was a clear day. He could easily see the beaches of Cheung Chau and Lantau islands and the little white houses scattered over the sun-browned hills. Leaning on the window ledge, he let his eyes focus unseeingly on the white oblong that was the Trappist monastery ten miles away on Lantau while he thought about Helen's return. I am numb to her, he thought. Accepting because I can't reject. Helen's letter, grey and grim as their life together, came back to him. *If I could think of a way out I'd take it.* Then, with a surge of hope, Mila's face superimposed itself over the remembered words, which for some reason he saw as white upon a grey background. A way out, a way out. He turned to Ah Wong at last, shrugging off hopes and fears till after the trial. 'Are you going to Canton this year?'

She was peering inside the cupboards, pressing her lips together and frowning. 'Let them stop killing each other first.'

Crown Counsel What in your view was the cause of death?

Witness The prime cause of death was a ruptured kidney together with shock and haemorrhage from multiple wounds.

Counsel How were these wounds caused?

Witness The bruises on the body were consistent with kicking by persons wearing heavy boots. Those about the head and face, which were not fatal, could have been caused by any blunt instrument, such as a policeman's baton or revolver.

Counsel It is important to fix the time at which in your opinion the fatal injuries were sustained.

Witness In my opinion all the injuries were sustained at about the same time, between five and twenty-four hours preceding the time of death.

Defence Counsel Did you at any time before or after you arrested him assault the deceased?

Accused He became violent when he entered the van and I assisted the corporal in restraining him.

Counsel How did you restrain him? Forcibly?

Accused It was necessary to strike him with the butt of my gun as he was trying to seize the corporal's gun. I hit him two or three times on the head while he was struggling with the corporal.

Counsel Did you strike or kick the deceased at any other time in any other way, apart from the three blows with your gun?

Accused Apart from the two or three times with my gun, not at all.

Counsel Did the corporal strike or kick him in your presence?

Accused The corporal did not strike him. He was wrestling with him to prevent the deceased getting at his gun.

Counsel What did the deceased do after you had struck him?

Accused He sat down and we handcuffed his hands behind his back.

Counsel Did lie fall down? Did he lose consciousness?

Witness No.

Counsel When did the deceased leave your custody?

Accused He was charged at the police station within one hour of arrest.

Defence Counsel About what time did all this take place, Mr Johnston?

Witness About half past ten or eleven.

Counsel So it was dark?

Witness The street lamps were on.

Counsel I put it to you that it was too dark for you to be able to distinguish one number from another on a policeman's shoulder several yards away.

Witness I was certain that I had the right number.

Counsel How could you tell from outside a van the doors of which were shut that the accused were assaulting the deceased rather than restraining him from attempting to seize their weapons?

Witness He was not resisting arrest when he went into the van. And the corporal kicked him on the way in. And then I heard a European voice saying 'Put the boot in again' in Cantonese.

Counsel How did you know it was a European voice?

Witness It was bad Cantonese. (Laughter.)

Defence Counsel You were at the charge desk when the accused brought in the deceased. Did you notice any injuries on the deceased?

Witness No.

Counsel None at all?

Witness Perhaps he was bleeding from the head. There were many people being charged.

Counsel Did the deceased walk in or was he carried to the charge desk?

Witness He was brought in by the accused.

Counsel Did be walk or did they carry him?

Witness I did not notice.

Counsel Was he in any way mistreated whilst in your custody?

Witness Not at all. Not to my knowledge.

Counsel When did he leave your custody?

Witness When he was sent to court the next morning.

Counsel When was that?

Witness About seven-thirty.

Counsel Did he walk unaided or did be need to be assisted?

Witness I believe two other prisoners were assisting him.

Counsel According to your testimony, the deceased did not need assistance when he entered the police station on the night preceding his death, but he did need it when he left it to be taken to court on the morning after his death. Yet you persist in claiming that he was not assaulted whilst in your custody?

Witness I did not notice whether he needed assistance when he entered the station. I was not aware of anything happening to him whilst he was in my custody.

Defence Counsel Miss Chan, you were seated in the car with the window open and you were nearer the police van than Mr Johnston. Have you normal eyesight? Normal hearing?

Witness I see very well, I have normal hearing.

Counsel Do you wear glasses or contact lenses? Or hearing aids?

Witness No.

Counsel Would you say you were in a better position to see what went on outside the police van and to hear what went on inside it than Mr Johnston was?

Witness I was in a slightly better position.

Counsel A better position. Will you tell the court what you observed.

Witness I saw the accused lead the deceased into the van. The inspector had his gun in his hand. The corporal kicked him in the back. After the door was shut I heard sounds of someone being beaten. I heard a European voice say 'Put the boot in again' in Cantonese. There was a man screaming with pain. When they came out Mr Johnston told me to get their number and we both looked. We agreed what the corporal's number was. The inspector did not have a number.

Counsel Your Honour, I must ask your leave to treat this witness as a hostile witness. This is not the testimony given by the witness in the signed statement I have before me. Indeed it is the exact opposite of what I have before me.

Crown Counsel Tell the court why you have changed your evidence.
Witness I decided to tell the truth.
Counsel Why did you not tell the truth to the police earlier?
Witness I was afraid I would not be able to get a visa to go to London.
Counsel Why did you think that?
Witness Someone phoned and warned me. Before I made any statement to the police.
Counsel But what you have now told the court is the truth?
Witness Yes.

Defence Counsel Did you report this alleged phone call to the police?
Witness No.
Counsel Why not?
Witness I thought it was the police who phoned me. They knew already.
(Laughter)
Counsel Did the caller identify himself as a policeman? Did he say who he was?
Witness No.
Counsel Why should you think he was a policeman then?
Witness I thought it was.
Counsel I suggest that the reason you did not go to the police is that there was no such caller and the statement you signed earlier is the plain truth.
Witness I did not go to the police because I did not trust them. That statement is false.
Counsel No doubt the jury will draw its own conclusions about who is to be trusted. Will you tell the court where you have been for the past month.
Witness I have been in Shanghai.
Counsel Is not Shanghai a hotbed of what is known as the 'Great Proletarian Cultural Revolution?' Is it not full of dedicated and active communists?
Witness All China is full of them.

Counsel I asked you about Shanghai. Will you please answer the question.

Witness Shanghai is full of them.

Counsel Before you went to Shanghai you signed a statement telling one story. You went to Shanghai, which is full of active and dedicated communists, and when you came back you decided to tell the court a totally different story. I put it to you that you were not tampered with in this colony but in Shanghai, where there are many people only too anxious to get their own back on the police force here which is daily frustrating a continuing communist campaign of terror.

Witness They do not care about the Hong Kong police in Shanghai. They have enough troubles of their own to think about.

(Laughter)

Counsel I am sure you are in a better position than any of us to say what they are thinking of in Shanghai.

The judge began his summing-up by reminding the jury that they must put out of their minds all matters except those directly relevant to the case. Political sympathies or antipathies in particular must not be allowed to cloud their judgement. No doubt many rioters had performed far worse acts of violence than that with which the accused stood charged. But it was the court's duty to administer the law impartially without regard to what other acts might or might not have been committed by people not presently before it.

Turning to the evidence of the prosecution, he said that much would depend upon the opinion the jury formed of the credibility of the witness Chan, who had changed her evidence in the course of the trial. How reliable was a witness who by her own account had told a pack of lies in order to protect herself from what she believed would be the consequences of telling the truth? The jury would have to assess her evidence very carefully. (The judge will complete his summing-up tomorrow morning.)

POLICE GUILTY OF MANSLAUGHTER
NINE YEARS FOR INSPECTOR. CORPORAL GETS FIVE

Two policemen, a European inspector and a Chinese corporal, were today found guilty of the manslaughter of a man who died after being arrested in a riot last July. The jury took one and a half hours to reach its verdict after hearing evidence for four days. A dramatic highlight of the trial was a change of evidence by one of the witnesses originally brought forward by the defence. Miss Mila Chan changed her testimony in the witness box, claiming that she had made a false statement to the police because an anonymous phone call had warned her not to tell the truth.

Passing sentence, the judge said he had taken into account the strong provocation under which the two men had acted but he had no alternative except to sentence them to long terms of imprisonment. It was unacceptable that any member of the police force should deny the very values which the force as a whole was patiently and courageously defending in the face of violent, persistent and cowardly attacks by those bent on undermining the orderly fabric of society.

Solicitors for the convicted men said last night that an appeal would be lodged. (Full report on page four.)

'Your hair's tied up again.'

She was loosening it already, turning her head and smiling as he pulled her close and kissed her throat. 'It is because the Anti-Corruption Branch has just been here. I have been trying to look demure.' She shook her hair free and put her arms round him. 'Is that better?'

'I have to get used to you again.' He had his eyes closed, feeling her cheek with his own. It was his body rather than his mind that seemed to remember her, feeling a sudden warmth of familiarity.

She pushed the door shut behind him.

He still held her, not kissing her, only feeling her breathing against him. 'They should've stayed.' He opened his eyes slowly to look at her face.

'The anti-corruption men?' Her eyes smiled, travelling over his face too, reassuring and remembering.

'Mm. I'm planning to corrupt your innocence before long. They might have learned something.' He held her at arm's length for a moment. 'Is that what you were thinking about, before the trial? Whether to change your evidence?'

'Yes, amongst other things.'

'What made you change, Mila?'

'I do not know.' She shrugged. 'I just did not want to go through with it any more ...' She led him into the room. 'Perhaps because of my father...'

'Your father?'

'He was dead already when I got there. I looked at him in his coffin ... When people are dead, they seem so very small.'

He waited for her to go on, but she only shrugged again and smiled, as if she was apologising.

'Go on.'

But she slipped away, dropping on to the white goatskin rug. 'Look, I'm on television. I did this dance months ago.'

He lay down beside her, his chin cupped in his hands. The screen was too dark, the picture shadowy and flickering. The dance was a slow, flowing one, which seemed to be a hybrid of Chinese classical dance and modern ballet. The music too had a plangent Chinese quality. She danced well, and yet he felt something missing in her languid graceful movements. There was a lack of tension which just blurred each gesture and made her appear to be casually practising, rather than performing. The longer she stays in Hong Kong, he thought, the more relaxed and lazy her dancing will become. If she's going to dance seriously, she'll have to get to London soon.

'I wonder how many people are watching this?' He rested his head against her shoulder.

'Just you and me ... It is only to plug a gap between the commercials.' She stroked her cheek along his head. 'Do you like it?'

'Better than bad commercials, anyway. I wouldn't say it was better than a really good commercial, of course, but...'

She bit the lobe of his ear.

He turned to her. She looked at him steadily, smiling, into his eyes. She was wearing a loose orange sweater. A small pendant hung at the base of her throat from a fine gold chain. He held it in his hand. It was a piece of jade, old and well carved.

'I haven't see this before?'

'From my father. The only bit of jewellery he had left.'

He ran his finger up the chain till he reached her neck. The gold gleamed dully on her skin. 'Were you sad about your father?'

'Yes.'

'Are you sad now?'

'Yes.' Her eyes still smiled at him with that considering, reserved look which was almost the first thing he had noticed about her. 'And no.'

He looked back at the television, still stroking the chain and her skin with his finger. Her skin felt smooth and warm, the chain felt bumpy and cold. Her dance had just finished. A washing-machine advertisement started with a barrage of enthusiastic Cantonese voices singing a jingle set to a western tune. He leaned forward to switch off the set. 'You really ought to go to London or somewhere if dancing means so much to you, you know. Otherwise you'll go off, like me.'

'It will be harder now,' she stretched herself out beside him.

'Because of the trial?'

'The anti-corruption men said I could be prosecuted for making a false statement in the first place. Would not that affect my chances of getting a visa?'

'Bluff. You haven't had any more phone calls have you?'

'Oh yes.'

'You have?' He lifted his head abruptly to look at her.

'Three times.'

'What did they say?'

'It is one man. He always says the same thing. I had better forget about going to London.'

'Have you told the anti-corruption people?'

'Oh yes. I have been making another lot of statements all morning.'

'What did they say when you told them?'

'Nothing. They just took the statements.'

He let his head slowly down onto the rug again.

'Besides, I do not think I will be able to get a job in England now.'

'Why?'

'I have no contacts.'

'Reuben Sternor?'

'Reuben Sternor does not like to be cut out by you.'

He lay gazing up at the fan, stationary now that it was November. A thin rind of dust and grime had gathered on the blades. His finger was still stroking the fine gold chain round her neck. 'What really made you change your mind, about your evidence?'

She raised her head slowly and smiled down at him without answering. Her hair fell like a curtain round his face and the necklace gleamed, swinging free from her throat. He tried to catch it in his mouth, but she swung it away with a wriggle of her shoulders. He caught it with his hand, though, and pulled her slowly down by the chain till her lips were on his.

'Doesn't this thing have a clasp?

'Leave it on, Dimitri.'

'I want you, not your necklace.'

'Love me, love my necklace.'

When at last they were tired they fell apart and lay half-dreaming, while the remote world came slowly back to them. Dimitri's eyes and ears opened slowly. The incessant rumble of traffic drifted through the open window. The fan blades hung still and silent above their heads. There was a crack in the ceiling running along from the fan to the corner. He gazed at the four white walls enclosing them and felt the wooden floor hard under his back. They were lying half on the floor, half on the rug. Mila's eyes were watching him drowsily through her lashes, her cheeks were flushed, her lips full and bruised. His fingers were tangled in her long, black hair. They watched each other with eyes too lazily sated even to smile. The gold necklace had slipped round her throat so that the pendant lay on her shoulder. Despite all the jumbled noises from the road outside, it seemed very quiet in the room.

A strand of hair had strayed down her cheek into the corner of her mouth. He stroked it away and she, turning her head slightly, caught his finger between her teeth and chewed it ruminatively, her eyes still watching his.

'That was about the best half-hour I've ever spent,' he said slowly.

'Mm. Was it only half an hour?'

'I don't know. But I just can't get enough of you.'

'Mm.'

And their eyes closed again.

She was dressing when he woke up, pulling on her dancing tights. The light was dimming into dusk already. She had covered him with a quilt from the bed. He watched her in the half-light as she moved noiselessly about like a cat. She went to the window to fasten her hair.

'I was offered the chance to dance again, in Shanghai,' she said quietly, without looking at him.

'How did you know I was awake?'

'Your breathing changed.'

He lifted himself on to his elbow. 'Where are you going?'

'Ballet lesson. In Wanchai.'

'I'll come along with you.' He picked his clothes up from where they lay untidily on the floor. 'How do you mean, they offered you a chance to dance again?'

'I would have to be re-educated. It would not be very painful.'

'What about the Red Guards?'

'They are on the way out now.'

'You mean they're trying to make up for your father? The people in Shanghai?'

She shook her head, gripping some hairpins in her mouth.

He pulled on his trousers and walked across to her. 'How ridiculous people look when they're half-dressed.' He took the pins out of her mouth and held them for her.

'They wanted me to do something for them.'

'Ah. Which was?'

'To change my evidence at the trial.'

'Oh,' his voice dropped. He watched her taking the pins one by one from his hand. 'Why?'

'I suppose they wanted to have some propaganda to use against the British...'

'Is *that* why you changed — ?'

'They told me the British would never convict their own police. They wanted me to give evidence against the inspector in particular.'

'Why? To make publicity?'

'It would look bad if there was a lot of evidence against him and he went free. They could use it for propaganda and — '

'*Is* that why you changed evidence, Mila? Just to make a deal?'

'I told the truth, Dimitri. About both of them, the inspector and the corporal.' She looked at him evenly, then went on with her hair.

'But if the deal had been that you should keep quiet?'

'I do not know, Dimitri ...' She turned to look out of the window. The lights had come on in the narrow, shabby street. A stream of cars flowed slowly, jerkily, nose-to-tail towards Nathan Road. 'I do not think...' She was frowning uncertainly. 'I do not know whether I would have been able to go through with the other story… in the end. My father looked so small in his coffin … But — '

He put his arm round her suddenly. 'I'm sorry, Mila. I've got no right to question you like that. It was easy for me.'

She was still frowning. 'I don't know if I would have been able to…But anyway,' she shrugged, 'it looks as if London is out now, with these phone calls I've been having. So Shanghai is all that's left…'

He turned her round and pulled her against him. 'They wouldn't dare touch you now, even if they ever could have. Whoever 'they' are. There would be too much publicity.'

'I do not know.'

'Besides, there is a simple solution.'

She laughed and pushed him away. 'I know what you are going to say.'

'Helen divorces me on the grounds of my adultery with you. And you marry me on the grounds of your adultery with me. Then you could come with me to England — assuming I get a job there, that is …'

She pulled on some slacks and a blouse. In the grey light he could hardly see her face across the room, but he knew she was smiling, almost indulgently.

'It is a fiction. You say it with your eyes shut, and when you open them you will not say it.'

'My eyes are open now.'

'No.'

'When?'

'When you are not with me but with Helen and your children and all the … all the connections they have with you.'

He buttoned up his shirt and went to the door with her. 'And if I met Helen off the 'plane and told her I wanted a divorce?'

She held his jacket for him. 'You are not ruthless enough.'

'How do you know?'

'Because I am ruthless — usually. Sometimes I slip up, but usually I am.'

She had her hand on the door. He lifted it off and pulled her to him again. 'But if I did tell her?'

'When would you tell her? At the arrival gate? In the taxi queue? On the ferry? With your children sitting beside you — or would you send them off for five minutes?'

'Bitch.'

'Ten minutes, then?' A square of electric light slanted through the window from the building opposite and shone on their faces. She reached up her hand and stroked his eyelids down with her forefinger, first the right, then the left. 'See, they are closed.'

'But if I did tell her?' he insisted, opening them again.

The light glistened on her eyes. 'You would be sorry afterwards.'

Sometimes I say to myself, well what is it, Helen, what's really wrong? And I don't know what it is, I can't say. I used to think it was the piano and the children, but now I don't know anymore. It seems to be my whole life.

I have everything in a way. Two beautiful children, a flat with a view over the islands, a servant even. I ought to be happy, I ought to be grateful. I think sometimes I'll be punished for not being satisfied. But yet I look at the poor boat people in Aberdeen with babies on their backs, they live on the boat and they die on it, just a few planks of wood, and yet I envy them because they smile and I can't even smile.

Ever since I've come back, I dream all the time. I keep dreaming I'm in this place and I can't remember having really seen it before. It's in the sea and there's a long stretch of sand. And I go to this place quite often and the sea is all quiet, you can't hear it like the real sea. And then I'm playing the piano on the sand only it's in a great big hall, too. And I'm wearing a long white gown. Or sometimes it's a red gown. I think it's the Albert Hall. And the applause is tremendous. But then suddenly I can't go on, the orchestra sort of stumbles and waits and everyone in the hall stands up and gasps and their feet are in the sea. Beautiful clear sea rippling round their feet and they're all watching me... And then I hear Dimitri's voice saying, 'Where're the bleeding scissors?' and when I try to go on playing, the piano won't make any sound. I press the keys and it won't play... It just won't play, no matter what I do. And it's funny because everyone else can play it, the conductor plays it and the audience, people from the audience come and tap the keys and it plays, but when I touch it, the keys just go down without a sound...

She was sighing that bitter, exasperated sigh again, throwing her head from side to side on the pillow. He had had his back turned to her and lain still, hoping she would go back to sleep, but now he gave up and rolled over, sighing irritably himself.

'Dimitri, are you awake?'

'Mm...'

'How long've you been awake?' The flat dead tone of her voice sharpened his irritation.

'Ever since you've been making that noise.'

'I woke you up?'

'Wasn't that the idea?'

'I'm sorry, Dimitri ...' She was not sighing, but sobbing silently, her cheeks wet with tears. 'I'm sorry, I just can't take it any more. I can't go on like this... I'm sorry ...'

The curtains were drawn back and he could see the star-glittering sky from where he lay on the bed. He listened to her sobbing. Once he would have put his arm round her, but now he lay stiff, not even letting his body touch hers.

You are not ruthless enough.

She brushed his shoulder with her hand, sniffing and breathing more evenly now. 'What are you thinking, Dimitri?'

'There's a handkerchief under the pillow.'

She blew her nose unsteadily and dabbed her eyes. 'What are you thinking?' she asked again, pleadingly. 'Why don't you say something?'

'Just thinking.'

She sighed, and he sensed that his distant curtness was edging her to the brink of more tears or bitterness.

'I was thinking about peace.' He forced himself to speak, still gazing out at the infinite magnificence of stars.

'You never like it when I ask you what you're thinking, do you?'

'I like to be left alone sometimes.'

'Always.'

'Well, who started wanting to be left alone?'

She blew her nose again and pushed the handkerchief back under his pillow. 'I don't give you peace, do I? It's not very peaceful with me, is it?'

He had braced himself unconsciously for a sharp answer, or at least a reproachful one, but she sounded almost penitent. His voice softened. 'I suppose neither of us gives the other much peace.'

You are not ruthless enough.

'I'm sorry, Dimitri. Why has it all gone so wrong?'

He shrugged and sighed. 'You wanted something different from all this ...' He waved his hand round the room, meaning not the room, not the flat, but the whole of their life together. 'This wasn't what you wanted. And what you did want you couldn't get.'

'I wanted to play so much, Dimitri. I wanted it so much ... All my life, until —'

She was quiet for some time and then she stirred. 'And it's not what you wanted, is it? All this?'

'I compromise more easily.'

You are not ruthless enough.

'Is it bad, not to be able to compromise?' She sounded naive and childlike, as though this was a new idea to her.

He snorted. 'Who the hell knows that? If you get what you want through not compromising, that's good. And if you don't get anything at all, that's bad ...'

Again she was quiet, and he thought she was falling asleep. He lifted his wrist to glance at his watch. Twenty to three. He lay with his eyes wide open, gazing into the blackness between the stars, thinking I compromise easily because I never believed I could be really happy anyway. Not until Mila.

'You must be sorry I came back?' Her voice was low and flat again.

He turned away from her onto his side.

'Don't you wish I'd never come back, Dimitri? ... Dimitri? Don't you wish I'd never come back?'

'I wish we could unlive our lives and start again. That's what I wish.'

Dimitri paused outside the door. Waves of sound surged loudly through the heavy teak wood. It was a record of Chopin's scherzos, played by Rubinstein — one of Helen's favourites once. He pressed the bell and waited, looking down at the children's Japanese bikes propped against the wall. The mudguards were dented already. The narrow hall shook with the violence of the sound. She'll blow the speakers, he thought.

Ah Wong's eye darkened the spy-hole and a moment later she opened the door. She let him in wordlessly, a sign that she was in a bad temper. He walked down towards the study, where the record player was. Helen was not there. The volume knob was turned full round. The windows were rattling with the vibration and the cloth over the speakers was trembling like a chest panting for breath. He turned the noise down and walked into the bedroom.

Helen was sitting by the dressing-table, gazing at her reflection in the mirror. Not even her eyes moved as he came in.

He shut the door. 'Why was it so loud?'

She didn't answer, only leaning forward slightly as if to see further into her eyes.

'I haven't heard this for years.'

Still she ignored him, until at last she lifted her shoulders faintly. 'Was it too loud?'

He sat down in the cane chair by the window. The low winter sun slanted hot dazzling slivers of light through the lathes of the rattan blind. 'Are you getting ready for the party?'

Her lip twisted, puckering her check slightly. 'Party!' she breathed, and shrugged.

'Well, are you?'

'Yes,' she said dully. 'I'm getting ready for the party.' She leant forward again and he saw that she was watching him in the mirror, watching him thoughtfully, as if puzzled by what she saw. He glanced away, resting his chin on his clasped hands. The print of Van Gogh's *Man Sowing* which hung above the bed was slightly awry.

'That picture's crooked,' he said broodingly. 'Where are the children?'

'What?'

'Where are the children?'

'In the amah's room. Watching television.' She never called her Ah Wong. It was always the amah, a phrase she could inject variously with indifference, hostility or contempt.

He got up and sighed, going across to straighten the picture. 'They're always goggling at that crap. I'll take them out with their bikes.' He glanced back at her from the door. 'What time is dinner?'

She had not looked at him once, except in the glass. But now she did turn her head and he realised suddenly that her eyes were wide and tear-stained. 'Surely you know that, Dimitri?' she murmured reproachfully. 'You've lived here long enough to know that, haven't you?'

He took them through Pokfulam village, where a communist banner hung on one house, a nationalist on the next, and out on to the farmlands beyond. The narrow little tracks ran up and round the humps of the hills, passing white-washed barns and stonewalled cattle pens with tall deep-green grass rustling between them.

The children raced until they were exhausted, then dropped their bikes to lie on some bales of straw overlooking a herd of cows in a stone enclosure. The cows gathered by the wall to munch the straw which the children threw down to them. Only one did not amble across. A large brown animal, she lay on her side, neck stretched out, eyes closed, her flanks heaving for breath.

'Is she dying, Dimitri?'

'I don't know, Elena. She looks sick, doesn't she?'

As they watched, a young calf pushed its way out of the herd and wobbled across to the cow. Straddling its legs, the calf began licking the cow's face and neck. The cow's eyes stayed shut and she lay quite still, apart from the heavy labour of breathing.

'She's kissing her mother,' Elena said.

'It's a he,' Alexander snorted.

'How do you know?'

'Girls have teats.'

'Well, that one doesn't.'

'That's 'cos she's young, like you are. You can't see them, like yours. You've got to grow up.'

Instead of squabbling with him, Elena giggled self-consciously and jumped down from the straw.

The sun was setting over Lantau. Already it had sunk below the mountains. Their sharp bleak shapes stood out black and stark against the rose-flushed sky.

'Come on, kids, we'll be late for dinner.'

Alexander stood looking at the cows, frowning.

'Come on, Alex.'

'Dimitri,' he turned, 'can cows remember what it was like before they were tamed? You know, when they were on the prairies and wild and free and all that?'

The path overlooked the sea all the way home. They kept pace with an oil tanker cruising up the Lamma channel towards the harbour. Already the sea was in the shadow of dusk, but the white bridge of the tanker still glowed faintly in the sunset. The children were pushing their bikes now up the last hill. They had taken their pullovers off and tied them by the sleeves round their waists. He let them draw ahead and watched them. For some reason they put their arms round each other's shoulders and pushed their bikes unsteadily with one hand. Immediately below them, the lights were being lit in the village and the dogs began barking. It is a fiction, he heard Mila's voice. You say it with your eyes shut, and when you open them you will not say it.

'Missy gone out,' Ah Wong announced at the door.

'Where?'

She shrugged expressively and waddled back into the kitchen.

The table was laid for three. In the fourth place was a note.

Gone for a drive. Don't wait for me. May see you at the party.

Dimitri folded the note over again and again, until it became a thick little pellet. How the hell did she expect him to get to the party without the car? He threw the note into the wastepaper basket.

'Tell us a story, 'mitri.' Elena sat down and wrinkled her nose. 'I hate this meat.'

'It's sweet and sour pork. You know you like it.'

'Tell us a story, go on. Please.'

'Not tonight, I'm broody.' He sat, scarcely eating, gazing out into the dark at the lighthouse flashing on Lamma Island and the lights of a ferry reflected in the water, on its way to Victoria.

With two sentences I could finish all this. Why don't I say them?

Ah Wong began clearing away the plates, nudging Alexander, her favourite, to finish eating.

'Was Missy dressed for the party, Ah Wong?' Dimitri asked her.

'I don't know,' she shrugged again, disclaiming both interest and responsibility. 'She was wearing a long dress, yes. Cheongsam.'

'The red one?'

'Yes, red.'

'What 'mitri? Where's she gone?' Alex asked quickly. He was always first to sense tension between them. 'What's the matter?'

'Nothing's the matter, Alex. She's just gone out for something, that's all. I just wondered whether to wait for her or take a taxi.'

'You ought to wait.' Elena looked at him down her nose, severely. 'Otherwise you'll get shouted at. Besides, you'll never get there by taxi. It'll cost too much.'

'Hmm.'

'Dimitri, will you play me a game of chess afterwards?' Alexander asked. 'Please?'

'Mm?' He glanced at Alex's eyes, always serious and concerned. 'If I have time, yes.'

'Where's the party?'

'Stanley. Near Stanley.'

'I hate Stanley Beach, it's full of rocks.' Elena sniffed

'What time?'

'Any time after nine, I suppose.'

'Well then, you can play.'

'You get ready for bed first. Otherwise you'll be too tired.'

'Stanley? Isn't that where you were in the war with the Japanese?'

'Tell us a story about the war.'

Dimitri changed his shirt in the bedroom, stopping to look at himself in the mirror. There were slight shadows under his eyes and little creases just appearing at the corners. He noticed in the mirror that the Van Gogh picture was crooked again, so crooked that Helen must have moved it herself. Stupid childish bitch, he thought, but he did not straighten it a second time.

Alexander had set the board up on the floor of his room. Across the hall, Elena was playing with her dolls.

'You look nice 'mitri.' She glanced up at him approvingly. 'Is it a party for people from the university?'

'Yes, I'm afraid so.'

They began playing. Alexander thought a long time over every move, while Dimitri, listening abstractedly for the doorbell, made his moves quickly and carelessly.

'Check.'

Alexander had checkmated him. He smiled down ruefully.

'You thought you didn't have to try because I'm young.'

'Yes, I suppose I must've done.'

'Next time you'll have to try harder.'

'Helen's back,' Elena announced from her room as the doorbell rang.

Helen came down the hall in her long red cheongsam, acknowledging none of them, and went into the bedroom. Dimitri followed slowly. She was sitting in front of the mirror again, gazing thoughtfully into her reflection.

'Don't you want anything to eat?

'No. Let's go.'

'Where've you been?'

'Just for a drive.' She seemed calmer now. Her eyes were heavy with thought, not tearfulness.

Elena called out from her room as he passed. 'What sort of party will it be? Who's going besides you?'

'Only a lot of bores from the university.'

'Why are you going then? If you're going to be bored?'

'Because.' Dimitri kissed her good night. Because it's better than staying at home, he thought. 'Good night, Alexander.'

'Play me tomorrow again, okay?'

Helen spent a long time saying good night to the children. He waited for her by the door, taking the car keys from the nail beside it. Looking down at the phone, jingling the keys in his hand, he suddenly wanted to pick up the receiver and call Mila, just to hear her voice. After that inevitable listening pause, her slow, unhurried voice.

At last Helen came. 'You were a long time saying good night to them,' he said as the lift doors slid to behind them.

'Was I?'

'I thought you were never coming.'

The lift whirred down. Helen gazed at her face in the mirror again, frowning slightly, and then stepped out silently as the lift stopped with a slight jolt.

They drove in silence to Aberdeen. Police at the check point waved them past and they drove slowly through the thronging, brightly lit main street.

'The anti-British posters have gone from the Mao-shops.' Dimitri nodded at the China Goods Store, whose windows were displaying now innocuous photos of some visiting delegation in Peking. "They must be changing their policy.'

Helen glanced out at the shop without answering. They drove on past Deep Water Bay and Repulse Bay, then on along the narrow switch-back road towards Stanley. The sea was several hundred feet beneath them now, glimmering in the moonlight. The puttering of the engine, echoing off the narrow rock walls of the road, soothed Dimitri and made Helen's silence unconstraining. He glanced at her face. She was gazing straight ahead unseeingly, her eyebrows half-lifted as if she were thinking of something absorbing but very far away. With her upswept hair and in the dim light that did not find the lines in her skin, she looked as she used to look when she played at concerts. I ought to tell her about Mila now, he thought, quietly and naturally. And his heart skipped a beat at the thought of it. But she was so self-immersed, it would have been cruel to shock the calm of her absorption.

You are not ruthless enough.

They slithered round the hairpin turn to Stanley. Usually, she was nervous in cars, and drove very carefully herself, but not even the squealing of the tyres disturbed her now.

The party was at an old house on a little beach beyond Stanley. He turned off down the narrow lane leading to it and parked at the end by the sea. Dance music boomed out across the sand from the balcony and people were laughing and talking loudly, their discordant voices carrying over the beach. A few sampans and a junk were anchored in the middle of the bay, their mast-lights reflected in the water. Someone was swimming, trailing phosphorescence from his arms and legs. Helen stood on the shore watching, clasping her handbag with both hands in front of her.

'Isn't this where the Japs killed a lot of people in the war?' she asked quietly.

'They used to take them out in boats and machine-gun them, yes ... We could see them from the internment camp over there.' He was relieved to be able to speak to her without any undertone of bitterness.

She nodded thoughtfully. 'I thought so.'

'The sharks used to come in when they sensed the blood... Even after the war, they still used to come, just to this beach ... And now people swim here as if nothing had ever happened.' He wanted to go on, hoping vaguely, half-unconsciously, that an understanding of the past might lead to some ground of sympathy on which he could draw in the present and Mila. 'I remember my mother was teaching me German once, she used to do it every day in the camp, God knows why — '

But Helen had turned already and was walking towards the house. As she walked up the steps onto the balcony, strangely poised and erect, just lifting her dress at the knee, she might have been going up onto the stage to play. He remembered again the tension of those minutes before she went on, the breathlessness, the warming of her fingers, the fidgeting with her hair and her dress and then the moment when she would walk with apparent serenity and a forced smile into the lights. If all that had come off, would there be any Mila now? He followed her up the steps.

Frank Browning was talking to her by the loudspeaker. She had a polite smile stiffening on her face while her eyes gazed inattentively past his shoulder. Then she slipped away.

The party was for all members of the senior common room, but there were hardly any Chinese there. They had never taken to the barbaric custom of standing to talk and drink whilst nibbling tasteless bits of food. The few Chinese who would come to these gatherings, which were really like a village cricket team's annual social, stood about, uncomfortably, drinking coca-cola or orange juice, and left as soon as they decently could. Or else, Chinese white men, they aped Western habits extravagantly, got drunk quickly and behaved like caricatures of high-spirited British undergraduates.

Dimitri took some vodka which Ah Fong, the discreet and friendly barman, had poured for him as soon as he came in. With his deprecatory smile and shrug, Ah Fong blinked at him through his thick glasses and told him the party was all very dull.

'Well Dimitri,' Frank Browning laid his hand on his shoulder. "That was a good day's work you got done in that trial.'

'D'you think so?'

'Don't you?' His eyes were bleary already.

'I don't know, I suppose so. It's all finished with now anyway.' He moved away slightly, so that Frank's hand slipped off his shoulder. 'Have you talked with any more cobras recently?'

'They're all asleep now. Hibernating.'

'You must miss them.'

'It's terrible,' Frank smiled crookedly. 'Reduced to talking with people now. Much less congenial. They answer back.'

'Well excuse me, I think I'll go and make the rounds.' Dimitri took another vodka from Ah Fong, whose eyelids fluttered with a tacit understanding of his desire to detach himself from Frank's boozy camaraderie.

He moved from group to group across the smooth flagstones of the balcony, hovering on the edge of each one, then wandering away again. Millie Whiting from the History Department accosted him between groups.

'Come and have a dance.' Her face had the hard lines and slightly bulging eyes of a frustrated woman making a last desperate stand against her fortieth birthday.

'Not just now, Millie.'

'For Christ's sake, don't you ever unbend?'

As he took his third vodka, it occurred to Dimitri that he was deliberately trying to get drunk so that he would have the nerve to blurt out something about Mila to Helen. He walked out on to the sand. There was an unreal lightness in his body while his thoughts remained detached and serious. People were scattered in little bunches over the beach and two or three were swimming.

'Where's Helen, Dimitri?'

'She's around somewhere.'

'Going for a swim?'

'Too cold.'

He walked down to the water's edge. The sea lapped calmly in, hissing up to his shoes then ebbing back again, creaking slightly in the wet sand. He shuffled his feet gradually backwards as the waves washed further up the shore, glistening faintly in the moonlight. This is where the sharks used to come, he thought. And there, where that junk is, that's about where they used to shoot from. He tilted his glass slowly till a few drops of vodka fell into the sea. A libation for the dead.

An argument had started behind him. He heard Henry Flack's American voice, loud and belligerent.

'Hand it back to China, for God's sake. What have you British done here in a hundred years except make money?'

'What's anyone done here?' Millie Whiting's voice retorted shrilly. 'Nothing wrong with making money is there? I've never heard of an American who thought *that* before.'

Dimitri tilted his glass again. The ice slid out and dropped into the sand. Half-listening to the row behind him, he watched the sampans out in the bay. They had begun fishing, dropping their nets in the sea, then rowing slowly back, threshing the water with an iron weight on a rope to scare the fish into the nets. The weight smashed into the sea rhythmically and the men rowing, standing with a single oar at the stern, leaned forward and back in time with the smashing. A hurricane lamp hung over the side of each boat, gleaming on the water.

'... founded on the opium trade and even now most of the police force live off it ...' he heard Flack declaring.

'Why the hell d'you think the refugees swim across Deep Bay to get here, then? I wouldn't risk being a shark's supper to get here if it was as bad as you make out.'

'The people who swim across are probably misinformed.' Flack said stiffly.

'Well, where was the support for the communists this summer? Three and a half-million Chinese and only ten thousand communists at a generous estimate. Were the other three million four hundred and ninety thousand misinformed too?'

'No. Terrorised.'

'By the police? You must be joking!'

'Ask Dimitri Johnston.'

Dimitri turned reluctantly. The moon was rising higher over the hills behind the beach, bright and calm. He could see the bluish shadows of its craters easily.

'I say, Dimitri,' Millie summoned him loudly, 'do come and tell this naive young American radical the people here have no more interest in joining the motherland at present than the motherland has in getting them back.' Her voice rose so shrilly that it cracked.

'I can't answer that question until a Gallup Poll's been taken.' He swallowed what was left of his vodka, solemnly. 'And then I won't need to.'

'Oh come on, man, you were born in the place, after all.'

'If I had my jacket here, I'd have my wallet ... And if I had my wallet here, I'd have two press photos inside it ...' He felt that his speech was slightly slurred although his mind was clearer than ever. 'And if I had those two photos here, I'd show you them.'

'Go on.'

'One is a photo of a decomposed body from China, hands tied behind his — or her — back, minus head. The other is of a man who died in custody after the police beat him up in Hong Kong. You may remember that case...'

'What's that supposed to mean?' Flack tossed his head impatiently.

'Well, at least you'll admit there was a fair trial and a conviction against the cops who did it,' Millie shrilled.

'They'll find a way of getting them off, you'll see,' Flack said scornfully. 'That trial was just window-dressing.'

Dimitri had gone towards the house, but he could hear their voices still raised in futile antagonism behind him.

Someone was playing the piano, thumping out a piece of jazz. It was Helen. She was playing vulgarly, extravagantly, slouching over the keys and banging them down without feeling, unless it was dislike.

'Talented wife you've got, Dimitri.' Frank was leaning against the wall watching her, a beer glass slanting dangerously in his hand. 'Very talented.'

'Would you say so?'

'I never knew she could play.' His glasses were crooked on his nose and he kept smiling loosely.

'She keeps it dark.'

'Positively tenebrous.'

'She was going to be a concert pianist once, believe it or not.'

'What happened?'

'It didn't come off. Where's your wife?'

'Didn't feel like it.' He raised his glass to his lips, slopping some beer unnoticed down his shirt.

Helen stopped playing when she saw Dimitri, smiled a strangely warm smile across the room, then dropped the lid with a bang. She came and led him out on to the balcony, where the record player was still booming.

'I want to dance,' she leant against him almost tenderly.

At first he thought she was drunk, but she seemed steady and calm. They danced a few bars, awkwardly — neither of them knew the steps — and then she pushed him gently away.

'You see, I can be quite nice, Dimitri.'

'Yes, I know,' he was still holding her hands.

'Now I want some fresh air. 'bye.' She eased her hands out of his and walked down the steps onto the beach.

He watched her until she had merged into the dark. She's stronger than I realised, he thought, as he watched her walking with that same poise, unusual now, with which she first went up the steps. Perhaps she really could handle things by herself.

He got another vodka from Ah Fong. The clinking of the ice in his glass reminded him of a phone ringing and suddenly he wanted to call Mila again.

'Is there a phone here Ah Fong?'

'In the hall.'

Again the long pause between the lifting of the phone at the other end and Mila's voice.

'Yes?'

'Mila.'

'Dimitri.'

'I'm drunk.'

No answer.

'Mila?'

'Yes?'

'I'm drunk.'

'Yes, I know.'

'I'm going to tell Helen.'

He knew by her silence that she was smiling.

'I'm going to tell her tonight. She's okay.'

'Did you have to get drunk to tell her?' The smile was in her voice now.

'You don't believe I'm going to tell her, do you?'

'I believe you would like to tell her, but you won't.'

'Bitch. You don't deserve me.'

'What's the party like?'

'I'm there now.'

'Yes, I can hear.'

'It's awful. What are you doing?'

'I am in bed, reading.'

'Reading what?'

'Poems.'

'Chinese?'

'Mm.'

'Read me one.'

'Now?'

'Yes.'

'Dimitri, you *are* drunk.'

'Actually, I just like hearing your voice. You can read it backwards if it makes you feel better. Anyway you like.'

'You are hearing my voice anyway.'

'Read, or I'll keep ringing you all night.'

'No. It is sentimental.'

'The poem?'

'You.'

'I'll keep ringing.'

After a short pause she laughed. 'I will disconnect.' The door opened behind him. Dimitri changed his voice. 'Someone wants the phone. I'd better go.'

'All right.'

'I won't ring you all night.' He saw that it was only Ah Fong putting some empties in the hall. 'So you can sleep in peace.'

'I would not mind. I will not disconnect.'

More people were dancing now. He watched them as he sipped his vodka, leaning against the wall. Their gestures and movements seemed suddenly grotesque to him. They waved and wiggled and jerked, and yet their faces were vacant, their eyes blank. None of them's really enjoying it, he thought, it's just a ritual they go through, because it exists. Like most other things. And while he watched with tired, half-drunk eyes, the dancers seemed to blur in a haze and turn into some amorphous monster with wriggling limbs crawling across the floor. He shook his head and went outside again.

Two people were still swimming close to the shore and Millie Whiting was still arguing raucously with Henry Flack. He walked away towards the rocks at the other end of the beach.

The music and voices faded slowly. Now only the hiss of the sea washing up the sand and the regular splash of the fishermen's weights as the sampans worked closer into the shore. A shriek of laughter insulted the quiet suddenly, but the returning silence seemed deeper than before. How petty it all is, he thought wearily. How absurd and trivial. Perhaps with Mila it really could be different.

He started climbing the rocks, his shoes slithering on their smooth surfaces. As he climbed higher, he came upon a pill-box, relic of the Japanese war, its concrete roof half-smashed, old bullet scars pitting its walls. Chinese characters had been daubed on one side in red paint.

HANG THE RUNNING DOGS OF IMPERIALISM!

Some coils of rusty barbed wire were still stretched across the rocks above the pill-box, hopelessly placed there a quarter of a century before by men required to die hideously, in order to retrieve the Empire's blotted honour. He remembered again the corpses he himself had seen. Men of the Middlesex Regiment, when all their ammunition was gone they had agreed to surrender, only to be bayoneted or decapitated one by one as they came out of their pill-boxes with their hands above their heads. He turned away and went on up the cliff. Yes, how absurd, he thought again, the massacres and stupidities that have drenched every foot of ground we tread on with their blood. Even here, where there isn't so much as a path. Why do we go on and never change? And he thought of the two photos he had cut from the papers and put in his wallet.

Now he had clambered up to the very top. Sitting down near the edge, be could see the whole sweep of the beach, a pale radiant white now, as it came under the full light of the moon. Distant sounds of music and stray shouts drifted up to him and he could see the dark shapes of people moving and the bright light from the house slanting sharply across the sand. On the sea, the fishermen were heaving in their nets, the sampans gliding slowly and silently the length of the bay. The junk stood motionless at anchor. A hundred feet below him, the swell from the Pacific breathed gently against the rocks, a border of foam where it lifted and sucked back. Far out, the dark shapes of

Chinese islands, the lights of a passing ship, then nothing but the empty sea and the star-filled sky.

His eyes felt sore and tired. He lay back and gazed up. The moon was nearly full, so brilliant that it hurt his eyes to look at it. He let his lids close. Images of Helen playing the piano, of the bullet-battered pill-box, of Mila in the court-room and of headless bodies in the sea jumbled together mistily in his mind. His eyes opened again. The stars seemed to be lifting and falling as with the motion of a boat, and it was as though he could feel the earth rocking as it rode in space. Slowly his lids closed once more.

It was the sound of the junk that awoke him, its loud putt-putt-putt engine echoing across the bay. His eyes opened. He saw the sky above him, darker now, and listened to the junk's engine carrying through the stillness. He sat up, feeling cold. The junk was towing the two sampans out to sea, lights glistening on the black water from its masts and stern. The moon had swung over the bay, down into the south. It was large and red now, with a splendour more majestic than any sunset. A widening stream of light spread out from it across the sea towards him and he watched the junk tow the sampans across its path, black upon silver. While he watched, the moon swung a little lower, dipping into a bank of low, flat clouds, illuminating them with its soft, opalescent light.

He stood up, looking down at the beach. It was dark and empty. There were no lights in the house and his car stood alone, a blurred shadow at the end of the lane. He glanced at his watch. Twenty past three. Helen must have got a lift with someone else. He felt for the car keys in his pocket and began climbing down to the beach.

He did not feel tired or drunk any longer. The air was cool and clear and he breathed it in deeply. Down past the pill-box, forlorn in the shadows, down onto the flat rocks by the beach and along the wet sand. I'll tell Helen when I get back, he thought. Or if she's asleep, I'll write her a letter. He felt suddenly relieved and exhilarated, feeling now that he really would do it. He walked buoyantly, listening to the crunch of his shoes in the sand.

I'll do it and Mila will stay with me.

The beach was shadowed by the headland. Towards the other end, near where the car was parked, a log was lying half in the water. He watched it rolling and lifting gently with the incoming waves and he thought from the way it moved it might be a sack, not a log. Not another body from China, he thought with a faint sickening in his stomach. And then he saw it was Helen.

She lay half-in, half-out of the water, her wet cheongsam. clinging to her body. Beside her was an empty glass, which, he noticed with a detached curiosity that did not fully register till later, had been carefully placed upright on the sand. Her handbag stood next to the glass, neatly closed, and in her hand was a plastic pill-container, quite empty. Her face looked grey. It was just out of the water. A trickle of whitish fluid was seeping down from her mouth on to the sand. She's dead, he thought numbly as he knelt down. But she was not dead yet. She was still breathing. Very slowly and feebly, with a fluttering sigh in her throat, but still breathing.

FELT SHE HAD FAILED

A verdict of suicide was returned yesterday on Mrs Helen Johnston, the wife of one of the chief witnesses in the recent trial of two policemen for manslaughter. She was found dying on a beach last month after a party. Evidence was given that she died from an overdose of sleeping tablets. The dead woman's husband, Mr D. Johnston, told the coroner that his wife had been depressed for some time because she felt she had failed in life. She had been unhappy and depressed ever since she came back from Europe in the autumn, he said. However, he did not know of anything that had happened to make her more depressed than usual. She had seemed 'about normal' when they had gone together to the party. He had not missed her until three in the morning when he started looking for her to take her home.

'How are the children, Dimitri?'

'Better now the inquest's over. They've started to play again.'

'Have they gone back to school?'

'I wish they could — the term's just ended.' He looked down at his coffee on the little glass table and stirred it meditatively. 'It's strange, she had quite a bit of grey in her hair. I never noticed until in the hospital, when they were ...' His voice faded. 'I'd never noticed before.

She must have kept it hidden ... I wouldn't 've thought she cared about that kind of thing, but she must've done...'

Walking across Statue Square to meet Mila, be had glanced at the fountains, silvery-grey spray under the grey December sky. They had reminded him of the silvery-grey streaks in Helen's dishevelled hair on the hospital bed. 'I'm sorry, Mr Johnston,' the doctor had said with a blend of sympathy and reproach. 'If you'd got her here earlier...' and then a shrug. And now he sat opposite Mila in the cafe, while canned Christmas carols oozed through the speakers concealed in the ceiling. I must take the children to see the street decorations, he thought blankly. They always liked that.

'Dimitri ...' Mila lifted her coffee and put it down again without drinking. The cup rattled slightly on the saucer. 'Dimitri, I am going back to Shanghai.'

He had obscurely expected it, and yet his stomach lifted and sank despairingly. He sat gazing at the fine bone of her wrist and the curve of her pale hand as her fingers toyed with the spoon. 'I know,' he said flatly at last.

'I mean, to stay.'

'I know.. . I've always known.'

Silent Night was being squeezed through the speakers now, crooned in a sickly sugared American voice with the backing of a honeyed choir. Yes, I must take the children to see the decorations, he thought blankly again. He felt as though his body was suddenly growing old and heavy. This is the end, then.

They sat gazing down at the table while the crooning and murmur of voices and clatter of crockery washed around them. 'That is why I did not want you to tell Helen,' Mila started again slowly. 'You see, I could not give up dancing. Even if I could not get to London.'

'Tell Helen?' He glanced at her, smiling bitterly. 'Someone did tell her, anyway.'

'What do you mean?'

He glanced at her irresolutely, regretting that he had started and wondering whether he could still pull back.

'What do you mean?' she insisted.

He paused a moment longer, then shrugged and took out his wallet. 'She sent this to me,' he withdrew a folded sheet of paper from the deepest pocket. 'She must have posted it in the evening, before we went to the party. It arrived the next day, when she was dead. It's a good postal service we have here.'

He watched Mila unfold it and read the single typed sentence, with several sentences in Helen's childlike round hand scrawled beneath it.

DEAR MRS JOHNSTON,

WHAT DANCE DOES YOUR POLICE-HATING HUSBAND PERFORM WITH YOUR DAUGHTERS COMMUNIST-LOVING DANCE TEACHER WHEN YOU ARE NOT LOOKING?

— A FRIEND

Underneath, Helen had written in big round letters

This came today, Dimitri.

If you can be happy with her, it gives me one more reason to go away. I hope she'll like Alexander as well as Elena, but anyway everyone will be better off without me. If you had told me you liked her I wouldn't have minded, But it doesn't matter now, does it?

Mila's face hardened slightly as she read, an almost imperceptible setting of the muscles. She handed the letter back without speaking and looked down at her coffee, still untouched. Her forefinger, slenderly crooked, just rested against her high, prominent cheekbone. 'You did not tell the police,' she said quietly at last.

'I never meant to tell anyone.' He was frowning down at the paper as if searching for some deeper meaning in Helen's childlike scrawl, then folded it slowly. 'Above all, I didn't mean to tell you. It just slipped out. Did you notice they spelt "daughter's" without the apostrophe? Illiterate bastards.'

She looked at him with changing expressions shadowing her steady, heavily-lidded eyes. 'I am sorry, Dimitri.'

'You see you're not the only one who gives false statements to the police.' He tried to answer lightly. 'Anyone can do it.' But there was a tremor he could not keep out of his voice.

'I am sorry, Dimitri.'

'Be careful, Mila.' His voice still had that tremor in it.

'What?'

'If you — when you go back to Shanghai. The Cultural Revolution isn't over yet.'

'I am sorry, Dimitri,' she said again, as if he hadn't spoken.

CONVICTED POLICEMEN FREED
APPEAL COURT QUASHES MANSLAUGHTER VERDICT

The court of appeal yesterday quashed the conviction of two policemen, a European inspector and a Chinese corporal, who were found guilty last November of the manslaughter of a young rioter.

The court upheld the plea of the defence counsel that the trial judge had failed to direct the jury properly. Delivering their verdict, the Appeal judges stated the court was satisfied that the trial judge did not direct the jury's attention to a material point in the prosecution's case. There was little doubt that deceased's death occurred as a result of injuries inflicted on him whilst he was being held in police custody, but the prosecution needed to prove that the fatal blows had been struck by the accused. Accused had had custody of the deceased for only one and a half hours and there was a conflict of evidence as to whether the deceased had received the blows from which he died during that period. According to the medical evidence, deceased's death occurred between five and twenty-four hours after the fatal injuries were inflicted. This was compatible with the prosecution's case that they were inflicted by the accused, but it did not entail it. In his summing up, the judge had not instructed the jury to consider whether the prosecution had proved beyond reasonable doubt that the fatal injuries were inflicted by the accused at or shortly after the time of the deceased's arrest, rather than by some other persons. Finding therefore that the jury bad not been properly directed, the court had no alternative but to quash the verdict against the accused and set them at liberty.

Contacted last night, a senior member of the Police Benevolent Association 'warmly welcomed' the Appeal Court's verdict.

Lok Ma Chau, by the Chinese border. A European man stands on the top of the hill under the police look-out post and watches the little track below. The track leads past the red and white barrier, past the duck farm, past the high barbed-wire fence into China, where a red flag droops against a flag-pole by a white barrier. The man is alone. He is not a tourist and the Hakka women who usually pose for snapshots do not pester him. They squat on their heels and smoke in the pavilion, watching indifferently as he leans against the fence.

Beyond the Chinese border post, the road winds round a wooded hill, from which the man knows unseen eyes are watching him, and behind that snakes the dull-gleaming Shum Chun river. Beyond the river, the plains go on and on until they merge into the foothills of the brown-grey mountains that dimly bar the way to Canton. A shaft of winter sunlight splinters the clouds and glistens on the smooth cold surface of the river. The man shifts his feet.

The track he is watching is empty, the river is empty, the fields are empty and the heavily clouded sky is empty. Only occasionally he hears the far-off quacking of ducks, quacking together, melancholy, discordant, hoarse.

Then a young Chinese woman appears on the track. She is carrying a brown suitcase and dressed in trousers and a quilted Chinese jacket. Her hair is braided into two pigtails. Leaning slightly to one side against the suitcase, she walks slowly along the track from the British barrier towards the Chinese barrier, and she is the only thing that moves. The man watches her. He watches her all the way to the barrier. She stops and puts her case down while a soldier in a grey-green uniform talks to her. Then she picks up her case and follows him into a whitewashed one-storey building beside the barrier.

The man stands watching for ten minutes, fifteen minutes, half an hour. Still he watches, until at last the soldier comes out, followed by the woman. She is still carrying the brown suitcase, still leaning against its weight, and she follows the soldier out of sight again round the back of the building.

The sudden, metallic clatter of a motor engine echoes up the hill and then a grey open truck drives slowly out from behind the whitewashed wall. The woman is sitting in the back. The truck lurches over a ditch onto the little track and moves away towards Shum Chun, clashing its gears. The woman is looking back as the truck goes faster, back at the hill where the man is standing. But if she sees him, she does not show it.

The truck goes faster, bumping and lurching. The ducks gabble and quack, setting some dogs barking, and then, gradually, they all fall still again. The man watches the truck swirling a cloud of yellowish dust behind it and watches the cloud of dust drifting away to settle on the dry brown fields. The truck grows smaller, is lost in its own dust, reappears, then vanishes behind the hill. There is nothing to be seen or heard, but still the man stands watching, watching the watching silence of the Chinese plain.

The dusk is blurring everything when he turns to go, every shape and every colour, and the Hakka women who pose for snapshots have long since trailed off to their village huts below the hill. Everything has melted into a soft luminous grey that is itself melting into dark.

He walks slowly back to his car, an old and rusty Mini, gets in and turns the key. The engine is cold. It coughs and splutters noisily, waking the ducks once more below the hill. At their alarmed, strident honking, the dogs too start wildly barking again.

The headlamps flick on, lighting up the pavilion, the fence, the trees, but not the dark invisibility of China. The car backs, turns and moves away down the hill. The putter of its engine slowly fades. The ducks settle uneasily back to sleep and one after another the dogs lie still.

The Sole Bar, the same Filipino Combo, the same tawdry decoration. Dimitri sits at the bar alone, gazing down at the saucer of peanuts the same barman has placed beside his beer.

'Where's Julie?' he asks in Cantonese.

The barman shrugs.

'Good evening, sir. Want some company?' The same mamasan sidles up to him, fatter now, her eyes circled with thick mascara.

'Where's Julie?' He asks again in Cantonese.

'Uh?' She shows a gold tooth as she smiles in recognition, answering affably in Cantonese too. 'Where've you been? Have you been away? Haven't seen you for months.'

'I've been around. Where's Julie?'

'Julie Wong? She's gone.'

'Where?'

She shrugs, glancing down at his glass.

He waves the barman to pour her a drink.

'Thanks.'

'Don't mention it.'

She eases herself onto the stool beside him. 'We threw her out. She was chasing the dragon. Not reliable any more. Could've got the place closed. Boss threw her out.'

'D'you know where she went?'

She shrugs again, turning down the corners of her thin red lips. 'Some place. I don't know.'

'No idea at all?'

She shakes her head, turning her lips still further down. 'You want to talk to another girl? I got some nice new girls now, very sexy. How about that one, in the red dress?'

'No, I wanted to see Julie.'

'Julie's no good now. You'll like this one, I know what kind of girl you like. You try Cherie.'

He glances at Cherie in the mirror behind the bar. She is slim like Julie, but younger, very young. Her arms are bare from her shoulder, extremely pale and slender.

'You like her? I make a cheap price for you. You want to buy her out for the night?'

He laughs, a slightly grating, brittle laugh. 'What d'you mean by cheap?'

'See if you like her first. Then we talk money. I bring her over, okay?'

He watches the mamasan in the mirror as she whispers in the girl's ear, then leads her across by the wrist.

'This is Miss Cherie,' she says gravely in English, and sidles away, not forgetting her unfinished drink.

The girl sits with her hands clasped in her lap, half-smiling, half-pouting. 'How are you?' she asks in stilted toneless English.

He takes her hand in his. It is very small, smaller than Mila's or Julie's, with long tapering fingers. 'You must be very young,' he says in Cantonese.

The barman puts a glass in front of her and tilts the bottle, glancing at Dimitri inquiringly.

'Okay.' Dimitri shrugs and watches him pour. He lifts the girl's hand up towards the light. 'How old are you really?'

'Twenty-one,' she lies.

'Twenty-one?' he smiles disbelievingly. 'Here,' turning her hand face up, 'let me read your palm. I'll tell you your fortune…'

Your eyes are closed. It is a fiction.

About the Author

Christopher New was born in England and educated at Oxford and Princeton Universities. He lived for nearly three decades in Asia and was for many years head of the Department of Philosophy at Hong Kong University. He now lives in Malta and writes fulltime. His books have been translated into German, Portuguese, Japanese and Chinese. *Shanghai* was on The New York Times Bestsellers list for eight weeks.

The Chinese Box is the second novel in New's China Coast Trilogy, of which *Shanghai* is the first and *A Change of Flag* the third. All three are being re-issued in Asia2000 editions. Together they constitute a deeply perceptive study of the British experience in Asia with all its cultural contrasts, a study in which the lives of rich and poor, Chinese and expatriate, are portrayed from one generation to the next, from the apogee of empire down to its final years.

Best-selling fiction and non-fiction about Asia from Asia 2000

Cheung Chau Dog Fanciers' Society   *by Alan B Pierce*
'A rare read indeed. An accurate slice of Hong Kong life — touching on heroin smuggling, money laundering, corruption in the police force as well as in one of Hong Kong's most wealthy and powerful Chinese families — a thriller with a difference.' — *Hongkong Standard*

Temutma   *by Rebecca Bradley and John Stewart Sloan*
An ancient monster is imprisoned beneath Kowloon Walled City in Hong Kong. It escapes . . . . 'Page-turning . . . intelligent writing and suspense, suspense, suspense . . . thrilling' — *South China Morning Post*

Riding a Tiger   *by Robert Abel*
'Fisher is under house arrest and required to write his testimony as the result of the mysterious death of his friend Chen Tai-pan . . . . Characters richly populate Fisher's life. His observations are philosophical and heartfelt. A lively, upbeat and humorous look at Beijing life through the eyes of an unabashed Westerner.' — *South China Morning Post*

Last Seen in Shanghai   *by Howard Turk*
Murder and intrigue in 1920s Shanghai. An American casino owner is embroiled in a plot involving warlords, pirates, revolutionaries and smugglers in a city divided between the British, French and Japanese.

Hong Kong Rose   *by Xu Xi*
From a crumbling perch with a view of the Statue of Liberty, Rose Kho, Hong Kong girl who made it, lost it, and may be about to make it or lose it again, reflects, scotch in hand, on a life that 'like an Indonesian mosquito disrupting my Chinese sleep' has controls of its own

Chinese Walls   *by Xu Xi*
'Although simply written, *Chinese Walls* tells a complex and controversial story of a Chinese family. The author goes boldly where other, perhaps overly-sensitive, Asian authors fear to tread in tackling such subjects as sex, Aids, homosexuality, incest and adultery.' — *Eastern Express*

Daughters of Hui   *by Xu Xi*
'Their menfolk are arrogant, absent Chinese husbands who neglect their wives for even more arrogant parents. Their extended families are xenophobic, diaspora Chinese whose worst nightmare is the horror of their offspring assimilated with the loathsome *gweilo*.' — *South China Morning Post*

Chinese Opera   *by Alex Kuo*
'Kuo gave himself an ambitious task, setting his story of an American-Chinese exploring his cultural roots against one of the most vivid historical backdrops of the century.' — *South China Morning Post*

Best-selling fiction and non-fiction about Asia from Asia 2000

Getting to Lamma   *by Jan Alexander*
A young American woman carves out a place for herself in Hong Kong. To do so she must deal with an old flame, a handsome young Shanghainese, two babies and an elderly Chinese nurse.

Farewell My Colony   *by Todd Crowell*
A journal of the final two years of Hong Kong under British rule.
   'An intelligent and illuminating book, the stylish writing is itself a source of pleasure.' — *Asiaweek*

Cantonese Culture   *by Shirley Ingram & Rebecca Ng*
A guide to the etiquette and customs of Hong Kong and other Southeast Asian cities. The rituals of daily life — birth, death, marriage, and the many festivals that make up the Chinese calendar are described and explained.

Hong Kong, Macau and the Muddy Pearl   *by Annabel Jackson*
'A pleasure to read and an inspiration to learn more about a region that has a surprising amount to offer.' — *Asiaweek*

Hong Kong Pathfinder   *by Martin Williams*
Explore Hong Kong's rugged hills, forested valleys, reservoirs and waterfalls, temples and aging villages, long-abandoned forts and near-uninhabited islands, lead by this informative pocket guide.
   'Thoughtful and meticulously researched' — *Action Asia Magazine*
   'A boon for neophyte ramblers in Hong Kong and a handy reference for old hiking hands.' — *Discovery*

Getting Along With the Chinese for fun and profit   *by Fred Schneiter*
Schneiter delves into the lighter side of Chinese psychology and demystifies one of the toughest markets in the world. He explains when you should and how you can apply pressure, what to do and what not to do when hosting Chinese guests, and much more. 'Facts on China no degree of study can give' — *The Shanghai Star*

Red Chips: the globalisation of China's enterprises   *by de Trenck et al*
'A useful resource for anyone seeking to find out about the structures and operations of China's conglomerates.' — *Finance Asia*

Walking to the Mountain   *by Wendy Teasdill*
'Wendy Teasdill provides a vivid personal account of how she was drawn to Mount Kailash. Inspired by the beauty of the landscape and her admiration for the Tibetan people she met, she reached her goal.' — *The Dalai Lama*

Round   *by Madeleine Slavick & Barbara Baker*
Award-winning photographs and poems forming a meandering circle through Asia, through Hong Kong, Japan, Korea, India, Tibet and other countries.

Best-selling fiction and non-fiction about Asia from Asia 2000

Dance with White Clouds   *by Goh Poh Seng*
This "Fable for Grownups" is the story of a man who, turning 60 and having everything he could want, runs away to start a new life. It is a comic fable about the paradoxes of life by one of Singapore's most distinguished writers.

Water Wood Pure Splendor   *by Agnes Lam*
Agnes Lam transports the reader fluidly through the national to the eternal in her second collection of poetry. Full of love and appreciation for the people of Hong Kong and mainland China. "Some of Agnes Lam's poems are so moving they will make you cry." — ***South China Morning Post***

The Last Puppet Master   *by Stephen Rogers*
The time is 1997. The place is Jakarta. The 30-year New Order Regime of President Suharto is about to collapse. It is a story that journalist David Collins must struggle to understand. "The sort of book that James Clavell might have produced about Indonesia." — ***South China Morning Post***

Sergeant Dickinson   *by Jerome Gold*
"Few novels in any genre are as lucid, or as memorably spooky, as Jerome Gold's new book, Sergeant Dickinson. It belongs on the high, narrow shelf of first-rate fiction about the battlefield experience." — ***The New York Times***

Egg Woman's Daughter   *by Mary Chan*
A moving memoir by young Tanka child, growing up in a Hong Kong fishing boat, who learns to cope with blindness, hunger and the casual insensitivity of family and peers. "This is the story of a woman who rose above disabilities, poverty and disaster by sheer force of will and deep religious faith." — ***South China Morning Post***

Childhood's Journey   *by Wu Tien-tze*
"The title says it all. The discovery of a childhood trauma becomes an adventure of the soul. Elegantly written and movingly told, Tien-tze's novel is a journey for young and old." — ***Hong Kong Magazine***

Tokyo: City on the Edge   *by Todd Crowell & Stephanie Forman Morimura*
Coolly poised at the starting line of the new millennium, Tokyo is the dynamic epicenter of cultural contradictions, manic creativity and the kooky vibrancy so central to our times. This profile of Tokyo, the first in more than 25 years, is more than a guidebook. It is a work of literature by two fine writers who know the city well.

Lipstick and Other Stories   *by Alex Kuo*
This collection of stories, set mostly in contemporary China, plays with and explodes the intricate and often murky relationships between ideology, dissidence and just plain survival.

Orchid Pavilion Books

Orchid Pavilion Books is the literary imprint of Asia 2000 Ltd., Hong Kong publishers of quality books since 1980. The imprint is inspired by the *Orchid Pavilion Preface*, a treatise on life penned by Wang Xizhi, China's most famous calligrapher.

To quote from *Behind the Brushstrokes*, an Asia 2000 book by Khoo Seow Haw and Nancy Penrose:

> By 352 A.D., Wang Zizhi was 50 years old, his reputation as a calligrapher was well established, and he had served as a court minister for many years. In the late spring of that year Wang Xizhi invited 41 calligraphers, poets, relatives and friends to accompany him on an outing to Lan Ting, the Orchid Pavilion, in the city of Shaoxing, Zhejiang province. It was the time of the year for the purification ceremony, when hands and bodies were cleansed with stream water to wash away any bad luck. The group of friends and scholars sat on each side of a flowing stream, and a little cup made out of a lotus leaf, full of wine, was floated down the stream. Whenever it floated in front of someone, that person was obliged to either compose a poem on the spot or to drink the wine as forfeit if he failed to come up with a poem.
>
> By the end of the day, 37 poems had been composed by 25 scholars. Wang Xizhi, as the head of this happy occasion, picked up a brush made out of rat whiskers and hairs and wrote on the spot the greatest masterpiece of Chinese calligraphy, the *Lan Ting Xu*, or the *Orchid Pavilion Preface*. Written on silk in the outstanding style of *Xing Shu* (Walking Style), the composition contains 28 vertical rows and 324 words. It is a philosophical discourse on the meaning of life. Wang Xizhi's calligraphy in this work is full of a natural energy, inspired by the happiness and grace of the moment, brimming with refinement and elegance. The *Orchid Pavilion Preface* became the greatest piece of *Xing Shu* and, although Wang Xizhi later tried more than 100 times to reproduce the work, he was never able to match the quality of the original.

Quality Books

From Asia 2000

Fiction

Dance with White Clouds	Goh Poh Seng
Lipstick and Other Stories	Alex Kuo
Chinese Opera	Alex Kuo
The Last Puppet Master	Stephen Rogers
Sergeant Dickinson	Jerome Gold
The Ghost Locust	Heather Stroud
Shanghai	Christopher New
A Change of Flag	Christopher New
Chinese Box	Christopher New
Last Seen in Shanghai	Howard Turk
Cheung Chau Dog Fanciers' Society	Alan B Pierce
Riding a Tiger, The Self-Criticism of Arnold Fisher	Robert Abel
Childhood's Journey	Wu Tien-tze
Getting to Lamma	Jan Alexander
Chinese Walls	Xu Xi
Daughters of Hui	Xu Xi
Hong Kong Rose	Xu Xi
Temutma	Rebecca Bradley & Stewart Sloan

Poetry

Round — Poems and Photographs of Asia	Barbara Baker & Madeleine Slavick
Traveling With a Bitter Melon	Leung Ping-kwan
Coming Ashore Far From Home	Peter Stambler
Salt	Mani Rao
The Last Beach	Mani Rao
Water Wood Pure Splendour	Agnes Lam
Woman to Woman	Agnes Lam
New Ends, Old Beginnings	Louise Ho
An Amorphous Melody — A Symphony in Verse	Kavita

Order from Asia 2000 Ltd

Fifth Floor, 31A Wyndham Street, Central, Hong Kong
Telephone: (852) 2530-1409; Fax: (852) 2526-1107
E-mail: sales@asia2000.com.hk; Website: http://www.asia2000.com.hk